CHILLY COMFORTS AND DISASTERS

A RAINA SUN MYSTERY

ANNE R. TAN

To Alicia

1

HOME SWEET HOME

As Raina Sun Louie stared at the dilapidated English cottage, she pressed her quivering lips together. Her husband was right. The one-hundred-year-old structure in front of them was their best bet for getting a house in the downtown area of Gold Springs. If she squinted, maybe she could ignore the sagging porch, the broken windows, and overgrown weeds. The house's current condition was just the starting point to her dream house.

Matthew Louie rubbed Raina's back and whispered into her ear. "It's all cosmetic. I can fix it up in two or three months."

For an Asian man, her husband was tall, almost six feet, and muscular. He worked out daily before his shift at the police station. His gold-flecked brown eyes usually scanned his surroundings, looking for threats, but today he held her gaze. He didn't plead, but the softening in his eyes was the closest thing to a puppy dog expression on his normally stoic face.

Raina took a deep breath, sighing as she exhaled. She ran a hand through her curly black hair. They had been searching for a house for the last six months. Homes in the downtown area rarely came on the market, and when they did, it came with a converted retail space and big price tag, which they didn't need.

The location of this house was perfect—five blocks from the senior condo complex where both their grandmas owned units. Their grandmas were close enough to walk over on a beautiful day but far enough to prevent them from popping over at all hours, according to Matthew. Raina had her doubts. A mere five blocks weren't enough to stop her grandma. It was a foreclosed house, so the bank wanted to get it off their books at a bargain-basement price.

Raina's grandma had gotten them the lead on this deal before the listing hit the market. Once it did, there might be a bidding war. The house had three bedrooms and two-and-a-half baths. There was a finished attic space that could be a bedroom or office. Matthew was right. The creaky floorboards and windows could all get fixed. And they could remodel the kitchen and get rid of the avocado green 70s appliances.

"We would have money left over to remodel," Matthew continued. "And we can always rent out the attic to a foreign exchange student when we need extra money. You'll have your dream house yet."

As a former civil engineer, Raina knew this wasn't a two- or three-month remodeling job, not with her husband working full time and doing overtime as the department tried to figure out their staffing issues. "Can we ask Blue to help? Maybe we can speed things up with him around." She smiled, hoping he wouldn't take her suggestion as a mark against his construction skills.

Her brother-in-law was a remodeling contractor in San Francisco. With his help, they might finish in the two or three months Matthew had predicted. But more importantly, she hoped they could finish the work before they ran out of money.

Luckily with the financial assistance from her family for her graduate school—yes, she was the poor relation—and her multiple part-time jobs, she still had some money left from her grandfather's inheritance. With the purchase of this house, the money would disappear like water running through her fingers. She didn't like this feeling one bit. Money had always made her feel secure.

"If it makes you feel better, I'll call him," Matthew said. He didn't sound happy at the thought. His newly found relationship with his half-brother was still in the honeymoon stage, and it probably was still awkward to ask for Blue's help.

Raina rose to her tiptoes and kissed his cheek. "Thank you, love. That would make me feel better. I know how things are at the station. I don't want you to take on this extra stress without help."

Matthew glanced down at her. "There's no room in your apartment for him."

"Maybe he can stay in Ah Ma's condo?"

Ah Ma was the formal title for paternal grandmother in Chinese. Newly married, Matthew's grandma was in the process of moving into her husband's unit down the hall at the senior condo complex. She was planning to list her unit in the spring.

Matthew nodded slowly. "Ah Ma would like having Blue around for a while."

"What do you think?" Iris Wells asked, coming down the driveway to join them. The real estate agent had taken longer than necessary to lock up the house to give them time to talk. Her smile wobbled. "Isn't this the perfect house to raise a family?"

Iris wore a white pantsuit, which contrasted with her ebony skin. She was tall, towering over both Raina and Matthew in her three-inch heels. And after three months of shepherding them around town to look at houses, Raina realized the real estate agent had the patience of a saint.

Matthew glanced at Raina, signaling that it was her call.

Raina frowned. She didn't want to make the wrong decision. What if this house ended up being a money pit? "I don't know."

"I'm not a contractor, but it seems like the flaws are all cosmetic," Iris said.

"The rooms downstairs are small," Raina said.

"This house was built before they invented the great room with the open floor plan," Iris said.

"We can knock down a few walls to create a great room downstairs," Matthew said.

Raina turned to study the house one more time with less critical eyes. Once remodeled, the house would be perfect. It was the path to perfection that made her uneasy. However, Blue was family, and he would do his best to help save them money.

She gave her husband a sideways glance. Maybe it was the proximity to the grandmas and the police station, but he was already in love with this house. If the poor condition was no deterrent to him... "Okay. Let's do it."

Matthew kissed her. "You won't regret this. We'll have the perfect home to raise a family."

Raina returned her gaze to the house in front of them. A cloud shifted, and a shaft of sunlight glinted off a jagged windowpane. She shivered. It looked almost as if the house was laughing at them.

2

ELEVEN MONTHS LATER

"I need to ask you for a favor," Blue said, turning the disposable coffee cup around and around in his hand. His voice was smooth with a trace of a European accent.

Raina and her brother-in-law stood around the kitchen island. It was the only place downstairs that was relatively free of debris and other construction material.

The avocado green appliances were still functional but were energy hogs. The tangerine-colored walls were an easy fix. Luckily, they were on schedule, which meant she could have a decent kitchen within the next two months.

Her grandma had brought over an electric kettle and boxes of instant coffee and tea on the first day of construction. This thoughtful gesture had saved more than one strained nerve in the last eleven months of her house remodel nightmare.

Sebastian "Blue" Luc's mother was Italian, so he inherited the hazel eyes and olive skin tone. From his Chinese father, he got the black hair and the gold flecks in his eyes.

Blue was more muscular and solid than his brother, which suited his profession as a general contractor, while Matthew was lean and wiry with a runner's physique. They were different enough outwardly that it took Raina a while to figure out the two of them were related.

Raina hesitated. She felt like a jerk for not saying yes right away, but whenever a family member asked for a favor—no matter how small—it always turned out to be complicated. And in this case, it would impact both sides of the family if there were hurt feelings. Not only was Blue her brother-in-law, but he was also married to Raina's cousin. One side or both sides of the family would undoubtedly complain about Raina's involvement at the end.

Blue had not only given them a great deal on the remodel work, but he also came through with finding them significant discounts. She sighed inwardly. Familial obligation and human decency meant she had to help.

"Let me guess. Does this have anything to do with your dad?" Raina asked.

Blue's eyes widened. "How did you know? Did he get in touch with you about getting together for Thanksgiving dinner?"

Wayne Louie had appeared briefly in Raina's Las

Vegas wedding several months ago. Matthew didn't see him in the crowd. Since then, she had been walking around with this secret, waiting for the other shoe to drop.

"Is he inviting us to dinner? Or does he want to show up for dinner?" Raina asked, hoping it would buy her a few precious seconds on how to react.

Matthew wouldn't want anything to do with his estranged father. Wayne was an alcoholic who turned abusive when drunk. His apologies afterward weren't worth much. He had left when Matthew was still in elementary school. And one day, his mother showed up at Ah Ma's doorstep to drop Matthew off and never came back.

At the time, Raina was too young to understand the full implication of these events, but now she understood what was never spoken. While the scars had scabbed over enough for the man to function, her husband was not a whole man.

Blue shrugged and gave her a sheepish look. "Since Dad is coming from out of town, he's inviting himself over for Thanksgiving."

Raina grimaced inwardly. She had the option of either inviting her father-in-law to join her extended family for dinner in San Francisco or hosting it in her newly remodeled house. She did some mental arithmetic. If they were lucky, the house would be completed at the end of October, giving her just a few weeks to move in and get ready for Thanksgiving.

The timing was tight. It would be insanely stressful

up until feast day. And Matthew would not thank her for interfering. But even if a reconciliation wasn't possible, confronting his dad might help Matthew bury his demons. It might make him whole.

"What does Ah Ma think about this?" Raina asked.

"She said it's up to Matthew."

In other words, Maggie Louie didn't want to have to pick between her son and grandson. And Raina didn't blame her one bit. She should take her cue from her grandma-in-law.

"Let me think about it," Raina said.

"Is this a 'yes, let me think about it' or a 'no, let me think about it'?" Blue asked.

Raina ignored his question. She didn't know which answer would correctly describe how she felt. "We both know how Matthew feels about this. I don't see him agreeing to it."

"We don't have to tell Matthew about it until the day before. If you give him a warning, he will call the whole thing off."

Raina shook her head. Her loyalty lay with her husband. "I'm not walking around with this secret for the next few weeks." Wayne's presence at her wedding didn't count. By the time she had pointed out the corner of the chapel to Matthew, her father-in-law had left.

"It's—"

Bam!

The wall between the kitchen and living room shook. Dust floated in the air.

Raina's eyes widened, and she grabbed hold of the kitchen island. What was that? An earthquake? But the ground felt steady enough underneath her feet.

Blue set his mug on the kitchen island. "If those numbskulls started tearing down the wall..." He picked up his hard hat and strode toward the entryway to the hall.

Bam! Bam!

Raina jumped at the noise and ran after him. A sudden spike in adrenaline caused her heart to beat more rapidly. So no earthquake, but a laborer who didn't know how to follow directions. Yikes! Depending on the damage, this might blow their already tight budget.

Blue skidded to a stop at the entryway to the living room. Technically, the room was probably called a parlor more than a hundred years ago. His mouth opened and closed twice without uttering a sound.

Raina followed his lead and stopped at the entryway. She peered in, and her jaw dropped.

The head of a sledgehammer was wedged into the drywall. Po Po held onto the handle with both hands and a foot braced against the wall, pulling at it with all her strength. Instead of safety glasses, she had on swimming goggles. A fine coat of white dust covered her entire face and much of her upper torso.

Her grandma wore a pink hard hat with skulls and crossbones stickers all around it, a neon green safety vest, and black steel toe boots. Underneath the safety gear was a neon orange T-shirt and leggings. Her silver hair had streaks of pink in it. Even from a mile away, a person would have to be blind to miss her grandma.

In contrast, Raina wore a worn T-shirt and baggy jeans. She had on safety boots—left behind from her previous career as an engineer—an old hard hat that probably no longer met the standards, and safety glasses. Her curly black hair was tucked in a messy ponytail.

When Po Po caught sight of them, she let go of the handle and placed the swimming goggles on her forehead. It looked like two pairs of eyes were peering at them. She jerked a thumb at the grapefruit-size hole in the wall. "I got started for you. Feel free to take over anytime."

Blue gaped at her. Newly married into the family, he still tiptoed around the matriarch of the family. Unlike Raina, who found her grandma's antics hilarious, he didn't know when she was joking or if the matriarch of the family might be going senile as the rumor had it. He raised an eyebrow at Raina as if to say it was her circus.

Raina sighed inwardly. Most days, she found her grandma's antics hilarious, but today was not one of them. "Po Po, what are you doing? You can't just start demoing the walls without, ah, professional guidance." She didn't want to get her grandma's tail up in the air. Like a cat, sometimes, her grandma's ego had to be properly managed.

"The two of you just kept yapping in the kitchen. Somebody's got to start the work. Rainy, you can't finish in time if you don't put in the sweat equity," Po Po said. She gave the sledgehammer another tug and handed it to Raina. "Imagine the loan officer's face. Now take your frustration out on the wall." She stepped back to join Blue at the entryway.

Blue gave the senior citizen a sideways glance and took a side step, creating more distance between them. Yep, he was firmly in the senile camp. It was a good thing Matthew didn't share his half-brother's view on the subject.

Raina tested the weight of the sledgehammer in her hand. It was about twenty pounds. Heavy enough to do some serious damage, but not so much that she could hurt herself. She swung the sledgehammer, and it connected with the drywall. Dust flew out, and she turned her head, blinking and coughing.

When she finally could speak again, she said, "I thought this was supposed to be fun. The people on *Fixer Upper* always seemed to be enjoying themselves."

Po Po wiggled her fingers. "It's called TV magic. Do you think reality TV is actually real? It's still scripted." She bounced on her toes and stretched out her hands. "My turn again. My turn. I got plenty of people I would like to take a swing at." She stepped into the room and reached for the sledgehammer.

Blue's eyes widened. He stepped forward and lifted the sledgehammer off of Po Po's hands. "Whoa, stallion. We wouldn't want you to pull a muscle."

Raina groaned inwardly. This was exactly the wrong thing to say to her grandma. His tone was teasing but also slightly patronizing. While it could be fun to watch Po Po eat him for breakfast, Raina needed Blue to finish the house remodel.

Po Po straightened and placed her hands on her hips. "What did you say?"

Raina linked arms with her grandma and tugged her back a step. "Why don't we let Blue finish the job? It's not as fun as it looks on TV. The sledgehammer is heavy. I was worried about dropping it on my toes the entire time."

Po Po harrumphed and gave Raina a sideways glance as if she knew what Raina was thinking. "Only for you, Rainy. Anyone else, and I would kick in his teeth." She spoke with a fake Brooklyn accent.

Even though Po Po grew up in a wealthy merchant family in China and learned English from the missionaries, she could speak with a Brooklyn accent when it suited her. She probably learned it from television.

Raina's lips twitched, and she bit her inner cheek to keep from laughing out loud. She would love to see the silver-haired, petite granny bust a karate kick at her burly brother-in-law.

Blue lifted the sledgehammer like it weighed nothing and swung it at the drywall. Instead of punching another grapefruit-size hole into the material, the entire sheet of drywall popped out like it only had been taped in place instead of nailed.

He stared at the wall in confusion. "What?"

"Careful! The whole panel is coming down," Raina

said, dragging her grandma back several more steps until they were clear across the room.

"Grab the hammer," Blue said, holding out the sledgehammer and using his shoulder and hand to bear the drywall up against the framing.

Raina darted over, grabbed the sledgehammer, and jumped back to join her grandma.

Blue used both his hands to slowly lower the piece of drywall to the ground. He dropped it the last few inches from the floor, and it hit the floor with a thud, stirring up a puff of dust.

"What is that?" Po Po said, pointing at a blue tarp-wrapped bundle wedged between the studs of the framing. She stepped closer for an inspection and wrinkled her nose. "Must be a dead animal."

She nudged the bag with a toe of her foot, and the whole thing fell onto the floor with a loud thud. Her grandma jumped back. "Yikes!"

Blue turned ashen, and he pointed a shaky finger at the tarp-wrapped bundle. "Wha...what's that?" His tone came out squeakier than normal.

Raina shifted her gaze to the floor and gasped. The tarp had loosened during the fall to reveal a three-inch gap. And through the opening, she saw the first two joints of a skeletal finger. It pointed straight at her grandma's boots.

She swallowed the bile rising in her throat. A putrid smell seemed to envelop the room. "Don't touch anything. Let's get out of here and call the police."

3

A DIFFERENT PARTNERSHIP

I t took Detective Sokol and Officer Joanna Hopper twenty minutes to get to the house. The dispatcher had thought Raina was joking at first and then grudgingly believed the tarp sack contained skeletal remains. While Raina was the unofficial pastry chef for the police station, the staff still thought of her as the harmless little sister with her curly black hair, short stature, and pencil figure. She didn't bother trying to correct this assumption.

The more people underestimated her intelligence, the more freely they spoke around her as if she were part of the furniture. Without even being conscious of it, she had become a source of information to her husband about the goings-on at the police station, which suited her curious nature just fine.

Even though Matthew still held the official title of detective, he had been temporarily upgraded to a more senior role with his work on the department budget and the contract negotiation with the County Sheriff. Everyone, including Raina, assumed he was on the fast track to deputy chief after his boss retired.

Of course, this didn't sit well with Detective Sokol, who wanted to climb up the ranks in the department. He could be a doppelgänger for Danny DeVito with a pug face and stout middle. He was as equally height challenged as Raina. Fatherhood sat well for the new parent, but it also made him sloppier than usual and more prone to cut corners. He didn't have the experience or the energy to do his job properly. And he knew it, too, which could make him a dangerous foe when threatened.

Unfortunately, for Officer Joanna Hopper, she was his unofficial keeper. She was a willowy blonde with huge blue eyes and a cherubic face that reminded Raina of the fat babies in Renaissance paintings. Her role was to smooth things out for the detective and to pick up on things he had missed.

When they were hiring for the detective position, she was on an extended leave in New Mexico. Even though Matthew had contacted Officer Hopper about the position, she was too busy running the household while her sister was in the hospital. She didn't even fill out the paperwork for the job. It was too bad because she would have been the better candidate.

As the detective and officer made their way up the driveway, Raina jumped up from the stairs on the front porch and ran down to greet them. "I am so glad you are here. Where's Mathew?"

Detective Sokol stiffened, and Officer Hopper's mouth twitched with amusement.

Raina did a mental head slap. "I'm sorry. I don't mean to offend you. I thought my husband would be here at a time like this." Her voice sounded unnaturally high like she sucked on helium from a balloon.

She hadn't realized until this moment that she was counting on Matthew's strong arms to bolster her. This discovery of the remains in their home impacted both of them. She thought he would be the first on the scene.

Detective Sokol tipped his chin in acknowledgment of her apology. "Where are the remains? Outside in the yard or inside the house? The dispatcher wasn't very clear."

"It's in the living room," Raina said. "This is going to ruin everything." To her horror, her lower lip wobbled. Even if they spent the money on a loan extension, construction might still run over by a week or two. Surely the bank wouldn't want to foreclose on the same house again?

Officer Hopper gave Raina a sympathetic look.

As Raina led the police into the house, she mulled over what just happened. Officer Hopper had carried a torch for Matthew for a long time. She had only recently, and grudgingly, accepted that he was off the market. So her sympathetic look might have an ulterior motive. Raina didn't doubt that Officer Hopper would be in the wings, ready to snatch Matthew up at the first opportunity.

Raina rolled her eyes at her own foolishness. She was over analyzing things again. Instead of focusing on such a trivial detail, she should be focusing on this bigger mess on her hands. From the entryway, she pointed at the living room. "It's in there. You can't miss it. I'll be in the kitchen with everyone else."

She marched through the hallway to the kitchen in the back of the house. Po Po and Blue held steaming mugs of tea, huddled around the kitchen island. Their ashen faces glanced up expectantly.

"The police are here. They'll probably take our statements in a bit," Raina said, walking over to join them. There was no furniture, but it felt right to cluster around the countertop.

"Do you think they will shut down the construction site?" Po Po whispered.

Raina shrugged. "I don't know what the process is for human remains. The tarp looks like it has been here for decades." She suppressed the urge to shiver. If she were superstitious, this would be considered an unlucky omen. "The police can't charge us for a crime."

"Is it possible for someone to plant the remains?" Blue asked. "It's unusual for the drywall to pop out like it did. There weren't enough nails to secure it."

Raina frowned. It was possible. Given her role in solving several murders, someone from the killer's family could hold a grudge. Or maybe someone was trying to get back at Matthew for his work at the police station. Though they locked the doors when they stopped construction for the day, they didn't try too hard with securing the house.

But this didn't make sense. There were no disturbances to the texture on the walls. The bones probably had been sealed inside the walls for decades. Long before they bought the house. This wasn't an act of revenge against Raina or Matthew. It was another case of their ancestors falling asleep on their job of looking out for them.

"Whoever hid the remains did it in a hurry," Raina said. "If this person had access to the house, say like the previous owner, he or she would have plenty of time to hang the drywall up properly."

"It couldn't be the owner of the house," Po Po said. "I wouldn't be able to live with the smell."

"One of the workers?" Blue said. He flushed. "I don't mean one of my workers. I meant in a previous remodel job."

"I would never believe this was the work of your employees," Raina said reassuringly. "I wonder if the owners pulled a building permit. If they did, we could get an idea of how long the remains had been in the walls."

"Or maybe it was an accident?" Po Po said. "A few years ago, there was a story in the newspaper about a woman who disappeared. The bank foreclosed on the house and sold it to a couple. While they were remodeling, they found her body between the walls. It turned out she fell through a gap in the attic and got stuck behind the walls. Since she lived by herself, no one knew about it."

Raina shivered at the similarity of the story with her current situation. She didn't even want to think about the trapped woman and her last moments. "There's no gap on the attic floor in this house, and someone wrapped the body with a tarp. This is no accident."

Blue covered his ears with his hands. "I don't want to talk about this anymore. It's morbid."

Po Po gave him a sideways glance and mouthed "chicken" to Raina. Out loud, she said, "I hope there's enough evidence to identify the person."

"With DNA testing and forensics these days, there should be plenty of material to find out who the victim is," Blue said. "Maybe we might even get an answer by tomorrow."

"It'll be weeks to get all the testing done. This is not a *CSI* episode," Raina said. "I'm worried they'll shut down the construction until all the testing is done."

Po Po squeezed Raina's hand. "Don't worry, Rainy. I'm sure they will remove the bag of bones and let you resume construction."

"I wonder what's keeping Matthew," Raina said. She wanted to call her husband, but he had a meeting with the chief and the mayor this morning. She figured the clerk at the station would have left him a message.

Blue frowned. "He may not be able to come, at least

not until later. Isn't it a conflict of interest for him to get involved in the case?"

Raina's heart sank. Of course, it would be a conflict of interest. And her husband could be a stickler for rules at the oddest times. Her cell phone chirped, and she pulled it out of her back pocket. "It's Matthew." She tapped on the screen.

You found a dead body in the house?!

Looked like he got the message from the clerk. Raina tapped out a reply.

Technically, it's a bag of bones. Will you stop by?

The cell phone chirped with another incoming message.

Who's there now?

Raina replied.

Sokol and Hopper.

There was a long pause. The phone chirped again.

I can't get involved professionally.

Raina closed her eyes and rubbed her temples. Just

as she suspected. She put her phone away. "Matthew said he would stop by later."

Po Po mumbled something unflattering under her breath.

Raina agreed. They were so screw—

"Mrs. Louie, can you come to the living room for a moment?" Officer Hopper said, stepping into the kitchen and crooking a finger.

Raina glanced from Po Po to Blue. "Wish me luck," she whispered.

Po Po gave Raina a thumbs up sign.

Officer Hopper went back to the hallway but stood outside the entryway to the living room.

Raina joined the officer, peering in at Detective Sokol, who crouched over the unwrapped bundle, the tarp spread out. Luckily there was no tissue or cartilage left. She squashed the urge to gag. This was no worse than examining the bones specimens in her classes. "Is it okay for me to stay out here?"

Detective Sokol glanced up and struggled to a standing position. He limped when he came over to join them. "Did you move the remains?"

Raina ignored his question. "What happened to your knee?"

A faint blush rose from the detective's neck and stained his wobbly jawline. "I hurt it chasing after the twins over the weekend. It's no big deal. Nothing a little ice and ibuprofen can't take care of."

Raina suppressed the urge to say something about having a doctor look at it, but it wasn't her place to nag him. Given how understaffed they were at the station, the police force wouldn't want another staff out on medical leave. And judging from the way Detective Sokol moved, it was only a matter of time before he would be out for his knee.

"I hope you feel better soon. As to that"—she pointed in the general direction of the living room—"it was wedged between the studs when the drywall popped out. And then my grandma touched it, and it fell, and the finger popped out. No one touched anything after that," Raina said.

Detective Sokol pressed his lips together. It probably took all of his willpower not to say something insulting about Po Po. There was no love lost between the detective and her grandma. "The remains looks human. I've called the county coroner's office, and someone is coming out."

Raina checked the time on her cell phone display. There might still be enough time this afternoon to finish with the wall demolition. "Okay, we can go to lunch and come back to finish up after they remove the bundle."

Detective Sokol nodded like he agreed with Raina's assessment of the situation.

"Whoa! There will be no more work today," Officer Hopper cut in. "Until we know if a crime was committed, you can't touch anything."

"You're shutting down our construction?" Raina asked. "You know we have nothing to do with the bones. They might have been inside the walls for decades. Are you charging us with a crime?"

"We don't know what happened," Detective Sokol said slowly, glancing at Officer Hopper from the corner of his eye. She nodded at him. "If this living room ends up being a crime scene, we would need to process it. And no one is being charged with a crime...yet."

"And I'm sure Matthew would want you to fully cooperate with the police," Officer Hopper said. Her tone was brisk. Professional and authoritative.

"Of course we'll cooperate. But how long are you shutting down the construction? The bank can foreclose on us if we don't finish the remodel in time," Raina said.

Something flickered behind Detective Sokol's eyes, and he shifted his gaze. Raina studied him for half a heartbeat. No, he would not mishandle the case to get back at Matthew. He couldn't be this petty. Messing with a work rival's finances on this scale would be extremely dishonorable.

"Officer Hopper, can I have a few minutes alone with Detective Sokol?" Raina asked. Her voice sounded distant and unusually grim.

Officer Hopper's gaze shifted between Raina and her superior officer as if finally aware of the tension in the room. "I'll start interviewing the other witnesses." She spun on her heels and trotted toward the kitchen, clearly not wanting to get involved in the drama.

Once Officer Hopper was out of earshot, Raina whispered, "Youri, remember all those times I've helped you, providing you with clues to crack your cases? I have never once asked for a favor in return."

Detective Sokol nodded stiffly like he didn't like being reminded of his incompetence.

Raina leaned closer to make sure he could hear her. "Don't you dare mess this one up." She spat the words out like bullets hitting a metal tin.

Detective Sokol swallowed. "I...I don't understand what you're trying to say."

"If I found out you"—Raina made air quotes —"misplace any information, delay any test, or mess up on the paperwork, and somehow we can't expediently resume construction, you're going to end up on my naughty list."

Detective Sokol straightened as if offended that she could question his professional integrity. "I... I would never do—"

"Do you understand me?" Raina was shocked by the steel in her voice, but nobody, and she meant nobody messed with her dream house. They had plans to start a family soon.

Detective Sokol swallowed again. "I wouldn't dream of it." His voice came out a tad higher than normal.

"If you need anything, anything at all, don't hesitate to ask me. I want this"—Raina gestured at the tarp bundle—"wrapped up soon. I have a house to finish."

Detective Sokol studied her for a long moment. "What are you going to do about the angry spirit in this house? It doesn't seem like a good environment to raise a family." His tone was sarcastic.

Raina shivered as if someone had walked over her grave. He had a point. Something would have to be done to get rid of the dirty energy in this house, but at the moment, she had to worry about getting the construction completed first.

4

THE GAME PLAN

By the time the coroner came an hour later, Officer Hopper had taken statements from everyone on the scene. Po Po complained about her dropping blood sugar level, which Raina took as a hint to get lunch. She ordered an extra-large combination pizza from Pasta Romano and left to pick up the order. When she came back, the tarp bundle was gone along with all the police personnel, and the living room was taped off.

Raina felt a sudden flash of annoyance at the yellow tape. Her house wasn't a crime scene. "Where did everyone go?" she asked, placing the pizza box on the kitchen island. "I got enough food for everyone."

Blue passed around the paper plates and napkins that came with the meal. "I guess they were hungry because they left in a hurry. Does anyone else feel weird that we're eating in the house?" He sneaked a glance over his shoulder as if expecting a ghostly presence to be hovering behind him.

Po Po shrugged. "Not really. We have nothing to do with the bag of bones and how it got here. It's no different from eating at the cemetery after we finish worshiping our ancestors."

Raina tried not to smile at her grandma's practical assessment of the situation. No matter how outrageous Po Po behaved, she was still very much firing at one hundred and ten percent when it counted.

And what her grandma said was true. Chinese families often brought a copious amount of food as offerings to their ancestors during the Ching Ming holiday, where they clean up the gravesite. Then they ate the food afterward among the incense smoke and burned joss papers.

They ate quickly. There was no point in lingering longer than necessary at the house. Construction was done for the day...and maybe for the rest of the week.

Raina and Po Po cleaned up the kitchen while Blue loaded his tools onto his pickup truck. He planned to head back to San Francisco within the next hour. While Blue was in town, his superintendent managed the contracts in the city. Her brother-in-law couldn't afford to hang around Gold Springs when there was paying work waiting for him in San Francisco.

Raina locked the front door and said goodbye to Po Po, who got in the passenger's seat of the pickup. Before heading out of town, Blue would drop Po Po off and visit his grandma at the senior condo complex. As he backed out of the driveway, a Jeep came into view down the street. Blue put on his parking brakes and waited.

Matthew pulled up next to the curb and got out of his Jeep. He waved to Raina, who stood on the stoop in front of the house, but he strode over to the pickup. Blue rolled down the window, and Matthew leaned in to talk to his brother. Raina was too far away to hear the conversation, but either Matthew or Po Po would fill her in later. She sat down on the steps to wait for her husband.

When Raina woke this morning, she had such high hopes of finishing the construction in time to host her first Thanksgiving meal. Now she would be lucky if she could afford the turkey and pumpkin pie. The delay would cost them dearly. Short of passing the hat around the family, and being the poor relation again, she couldn't see a way out of their situation.

Blue finally left, and Raina waved from the steps. Matthew trotted up the driveway and joined her. He sank down with a sigh, slinging an arm around her shoulders. She echoed his sigh. They sat in silence for a long moment, looking at the green lawn with the tire swing on the old oak tree. If she squinted, she could imagine a child having a tea party on the grass.

"What's the game plan now?" Raina asked, breaking the uneasy silence. She didn't want to dwell on the image of a future child playing in the yard, especially if they ended up losing the house.

"I don't have one," Matthew said. "There's nothing I

can do professionally. They don't let doctors operate on family members for a reason. I would be too emotionally invested to think objectively."

Raina gaped at him. Wasn't he planning to investigate on the down-low? After all, he could solve the case and hand it wrapped in a red bow to Detective Sokol. No one would be any wiser. "You're joking, right?"

Matthew shook his head. "Joanna will make sure Youri doesn't mess this one up."

"I'm sure Officer Hopper is good at her job, but you're the best detective on the force. You can't sit this one out. It's our future at stake."

"I have to follow procedure. My job is at stake. We can always buy another house, but a full-time job with good benefits in a small town is hard to come by." He squeezed her shoulders. "I have to do what's best for our family."

Raina closed her eyes and rubbed her throbbing temples. Of course, Matthew was right. He couldn't flout the rules when it suited him. It would set a bad precedent, especially since he was up for promotion. "But what do we do now?"

"We wait. Until the coroner makes a determination, we don't even know if the remains belonged to an animal or human."

"It's human. And probably about ten to thirty years old."

"How do you know?"

"I've examined enough bones in my classes. There wasn't any tissue or cartilage left in them, but the bones weren't brittle yet. And given that it was hidden in our walls, this is a criminal case," Raina said. As the words left her mouth, her gut agreed with her logical assessment of the situation. A cold case.

Matthew grimaced. "I figured as much, but I didn't want to say anything. I didn't want you to worry."

"Did you think I wouldn't notice?"

He gave her a sheepish look, which suggested he was hoping she wouldn't notice. "I don't know what to think."

"What we need is a game plan. The remains could have been in the wall for decades. Detective Sokol doesn't have the patience to sift through old newspapers and files to solve a cold case."

"But you do." Matthew said the three words with absolute confidence. Though he sat next to Raina, his gaze was on the lawn.

Raina watched his profile, his jaw clenching and unclenching. *Okay then*, she thought. This was his blessing for her to step in. Even though he was off duty, he couldn't tell her to investigate the case because he was still a cop. And cops didn't go around telling civilians to solve their cases. A small bubble of pride welled up in her chest. She reached for his hand and squeezed it. There was no need to say anything more about it.

"We need to finish the loan extension paperwork tonight," Raina said.

"It will buy us an extra three months. Do we have enough cash to cover the fees?" Matthew asked.

Before the purchase of the house, she'd had a good-sized nest egg from her inheritance. The money in the bank had always made her feel secure in a way that her part-time jobs didn't. But now, after paying all the invoices, they were down to the last five thousand dollars, half of which they would have to hand over to cover the fees for the loan extension. Without progress, the bank would not be disbursing any more funds from the construction loan. They would run into cash flow issues sooner rather than later.

"Barely." Raina paused, choosing her words with care. "Should I ask Po Po for a loan?"

"No!"

Raina cringed inwardly. She figured this would be his reaction. Even though the Louies were part of the wealthy generational Chinese merchants of San Francisco, his family had lost most of their wealth decades ago after his grandfather's death.

Matthew had to join the Marines to get the government to help pay for his education. Like most Chinese men, a loan from his wife's family implied that he couldn't take care of his wife. Machismo didn't just apply to Mexican men.

He took a deep breath. "No," he said more calmly. "I'll do more over time. After all, I don't need to do work at the house in the evenings anymore. There is plenty to do with Youri and Joanne working on this case." The police force was small enough that a shift in workload had a ripple effect on everyone else.

She wanted to offer to pick up more shifts at the

Venus Café or ask one of the professors for more hours on campus, but her time was probably best served bird-dogging this cold case. Time was money when it came to construction.

"Rainy," Matthew said. He met her eyes and held them. His gold-flecked brown eyes softened, and frown lines appeared on his forehead. "Nothing is worth the risk of losing you. Not even this house." He kissed the top of her head. "Take care of yourself."

Raina swallowed the sudden lump in her throat. She knew exactly how he felt. Every morning, as he walked out the door for his shift at the station, she prayed for his safety. Being the wife of a small-town cop would probably take years off her life.

While they didn't have gangs and other organized crime in their small community, it didn't mean the criminals weren't equally as dangerous. While it was the sheriff's jurisdiction to follow up on calls for those properties outside of town, most of the time, the Gold Springs Police responded because they were just plain closer.

Many of these criminals, especially those that lived in the unincorporated area, often had an armory on their property. One never knew what to expect on one of these calls. In many ways, Raina was thankful Matthew had been working on the budget and contract negotiations for the last few months.

"Don't worry. I wouldn't give you the pleasure of dancing naked on my grave," Raina said.

Matthew chuckled just as she hoped he would. "At

the rate things are going, your grandma would be the one dancing."

"Yeah, she'll live forever."

"I understand wearing a safety vest when you're around heavy equipment, but the neon outfit too? Where does she get her clothes?"

Raina shrugged. "My grandma on the internet with a credit card can be a scary thing."

They fell silent for several long moments. Raina's thoughts drifted back to her conversation with Detective Youri. She practically threatened him. Maybe she should say something to Matthew about it. After all, she was counting on Detective Sokol's silence, but if he said something about the incident, things could turn ugly fast. And Matthew needed to know before he got blindsided at the station.

Raina gave her husband a sideways glance. She wished she could smooth the frown lines and take away the tension. The poor man already had a lot on his plate. She couldn't spring this on him today, along with the Thanksgiving dinner with his estranged father. Tomorrow. She would tell him tomorrow.

5

TOO CLOSE FOR COMFORT

The Venus Cafe was quiet, except for Po Po's Posse Club meeting. The senior citizens took over the leather reading chairs by the fireplace with cups of teas and plates of pastries. At Raina's suggestion, the cafe had expanded its tea selection beyond Lipton to some herbal blends and white tea for their older clientele who couldn't tolerate caffeine. She wasn't sure when the club moved their weekly meeting to the cafe, but the owners didn't mind. The club brought in business during the dead hours between lunch and the early dinner crowd.

When Raina first started the job, she often felt a secret thrill. Some of the town elders thought the cafe a disgrace because of the floor-to-ceiling painted murals of lounging naked nymphs and frolicking men. Only the strategic placement of leaves, berries, and flowing hair kept the paintings from being obscene. However, like most things, constant exposure led to numbness. The Venus Cafe became a place of employment rather than enjoyment. She wasn't sure if she loved the change or not.

Today's Posse Club meeting was relatively small by the usual standards. Several of their members were out of town, leaving Po Po, Frank Small, and Maggie Louie Small to huddle around the fireplace. Frank and Maggie, Matthew's grandma, recently got married. Raina thought the couple was sweet, but her husband closed his eyes each time the two of them publicly displayed their affection by holding hands or kissing cheeks. Sometimes Matthew could be so immature.

The three of them spoke in hushed tones and occasionally threw glances at Raina. She ignored them. She knew exactly what they wanted to talk to her about, but she wasn't sure where to start either.

Raina sat at a table by the cash register, rolling utensils into napkins. As with all restaurants, a thousand small tasks had to be done during the lull times. There were condiments and napkin containers that needed to be refilled, surfaces to wipe down, and things to pick up.

Po Po stood and sauntered over to join Raina. She pulled out a chair and made herself at home. "So, Sherlock, when do we start shaking people down?"

Raina suppressed a grin. She raised an eyebrow instead. Sitting on the sidelines and waiting for Detective Sokol to bumble his way through the investigation wasn't an option. Her dream house and finances were at stake. It was too important to not jump in full tilt. "For what, Watson?"

"Don't you think we should do something? The police would compile a list of missing people in their database for the last few years, but they probably won't give us a copy."

"I know," Raina said.

"Can you use your wiles on Matthew to get him to show you the list?" Po Po asked.

Raina laughed. "Not when he can get the milk for free."

Po Po rolled her eyes. "You have to get some skimpy lingerie, girl. Men don't drool over underwear with holes in them."

Raina didn't think her husband cared one way or another as long as the underwear came off. "Maybe we should check with the library to see if they have newspaper archives about missing people in the area? From what I can tell from the skeletal hand, the remains are probably closer to thirty years old."

Po Po made a face. "I hate looking at microfiche. It takes so much time."

"What's that? Wouldn't the records be in a searchable database?"

Po Po burst out laughing. The Smalls glanced over, exchanged a look, and joined them at the table.

"What's so funny?" Maggie asked, turning an ear toward the source of the laughter. Her visual impairment had stabilized this past year, but she still had a habit of using her ears to follow the conversation rather than her eyes.

"Rainy is asking what a microfiche is," Po Po said, grinning.

Raina knew what a microfiche was. There was an ancient old dusty microfiche machine in the basement of the San Francisco Public Library. She never operated one, but it probably didn't take a degree in rocket science to figure it out. But she didn't want to ruin her grandma's joke, so she stared around the table, hoping to prolong the ribbing.

"In the old days, before the internet, the newspapers were archived on a film called microfiche," Frank said. "A machine projects the film on a screen so you can read the old papers."

Raina continued to blink at them. Time for the ultimate millennial topper. She gave them a puzzled look, wrinkling her nose. "I'm not sure why we need to look at the 'microfilm' when we can search the internet. I'm sure the records are online by now."

The Posse Club burst out into laughter. The corner of Raina's mouth twitched, and she glanced down at the napkins and utensils to hide her amusement. And people thought millennials had a poor attitude against ageism. If being the butt of a small joke made these retirees happy, it was fine by her. They had saved her bacon the few times she found herself in a sticky situation.

"Har-har," Raina said, a wide grin on her face. "I

guess I'll have to leave this task to you. I don't know how to work the machine."

"What about us?" Maggie asked, leaning forward in her seat.

Raina raced through the possibilities in her mind. With Maggie's visual impairment, she couldn't very well squint at the microfiche. What could she do that would make her feel useful but kept her somewhere safe?

"Why don't you ask around the senior center to see if anyone remembers any disappearances from twenty or thirty years ago? They might have better information than what's in the newspapers," she said.

Maggie and Frank nodded. "We're on it, Sherlock."

"I have to drop off some paperwork at the bank, and then I'm calling my real estate agent," Raina said. "She might have some information about the former owners. And if that doesn't yield anything useful, I will stop by the building permit desk."

"Let's synchronize our watches," Po Po said, thrusting the hand with the smartwatch on it onto the middle of the table.

Raina thrust her hand to join the others even though she didn't have a watch. She wasn't sure when she became the de facto leader when it came to murder investigations for the Posse Club, but she was glad to have some semblance of control over her grandma. The last thing Raina needed was for Po Po to go rogue and do something totally in character and get thrown into a holding cell. She would hate to have to choose between her husband and her grandma.

RAINA HANDED over the paperwork for the construction loan extension to the bank vice president. She didn't want to think about the fee or what would happen if they didn't get the remodel done on time.

Chase McKenna studied the paperwork, slowly flipping through the stack and making sure Raina and her husband had crossed every "t" and dotted every "i." Their regular loan officer was on a European vacation, so his boss was filling in.

The bank vice president wore a three-piece pinstripe suit with a red silk handkerchief in his pocket. He was in his fifties with a bald plate. What remained of his brown hair was streaked with gray. His set of dazzling white teeth probably cost more than Raina's loan extension. He was probably a former high school football star because he still had the jock air around him. The suit did much of the work to hide his softening middle.

On his mahogany shelf behind his matching desk was a framed photo of his family—Chase, his wife, and his teenage son. Next to this prerequisite family photo, was a framed photo of his son in his football gear. Were having pictures of his family a sign that he could be trusted and committed to helping the community?

It was an odd business practice she had seen in many businesses.

Raina sat back in her chair, hoping her impatience didn't show on her face. There was only one month left on her original construction loan and she still had to knock down the walls in the living room and update the kitchen. Or maybe she could live with the dated kitchen and remodel it later after she rolled the construction loan into a traditional mortgage. It wouldn't be ideal, but when did life ever follow a roadmap?

Replacing the roof, windows, and portions of the siding had taken a lot longer than expected because of all the mold and dry rot. She sneaked a glance at the wall clock. The building permit office would close in forty minutes, and she wanted to see if she could obtain information about previous building permits.

"What is your plan for finishing on time?" Chase asked, glancing up from the paperwork.

Raina licked her lips. Should she tell the bank VP about the tarp bundle in the drywall? He might not approve the extension if he thought the Louies would default on the construction loan. No one wanted to be stuck with a partially remodeled house.

"The contractor is bringing in more people," she said, hoping rumors of the remains hadn't had a chance to spread through the town yet.

"Why don't you keep the current layout for the downstairs?"

Raina shook her head. She didn't want to mention

that now they would have no choice but to continue. Half the wall was down already thanks to her grandma and Blue's effort yesterday. "We want to modernize the inside. And we want a great room for the kitchen, dining room, and living area."

"But what about the existing fireplace?"

"We planned to put in an electric fireplace for ambiance." She didn't bother telling him the hundred-year-old fireplace was disgusting, filled with soot and unidentifiable black lumps.

Chase raised an eyebrow. "Uh-huh."

Raina stiffened her spine. It didn't matter what Chase thought about her plans for the house. Once they were done with the construction and refinanced the loan, she wouldn't have to deal with the bank vice president again. "Is the paperwork all in order?" Her tone was brisk. She should try to be friendlier, but she wasn't the type to grovel.

Chase straightened the pile of paperwork. "Yes, it looks fine. We'll withdraw the fee from your checking account."

The peal of a Chinese pipa filled the air. The lute music was distinct enough to cause a customer in line to glance around for the source of the sound.

Raina jumped at the noise. "Sorry," she mumbled, digging in her purse and pulling out the device. It was from Po Po. She dismissed the call. She doubted her grandma had found something in the microfiche this quickly.

She focused her attention back at Chase, wanting

to ask if it was possible to do a second loan extension. His inscrutable expression wasn't one that welcomed confidences or chatter. He wasn't the right person to ask. And besides, now wasn't the time for this discussion. She rose from the chair, sticking out her hand for a good-bye handshake. "Thank you, Chase, for your time."

"Whoa! I still have a few more questions," Chase said, slipping the paperwork into a manila folder.

Raina sank back onto the chair, clutching the cell phone in her hand. It vibrated, indicating that her grandma had left a message. "I need to get to the building permit office. They close in twenty minutes."

"This will just take another minute," Chase said. "I want to make sure you're clear on the terms of this extension. If you don't finish the construction on time, we'll have to foreclose on your house."

Raina gasped, and her eyes widened. She knew foreclosure was a possibility, but to hear it said out loud made it a reality. A foreclosure could wipe them out. It would take them years to save up for another down payment. Her heart raced at the thought, and sweat beaded at the small of her back.

What if they had to choose between saving for another house or having children? Matthew liked following a timetable. Life's milestones were like engravings on concrete. Marriage, house, and children in the proper order. Would staying at a rental make him feel like a failure? Like he couldn't provide for them? Chinese males were unpredictable sometimes because the old-fashioned ideas came out in the oddest situations.

Chase's brows furrowed. "I hope you and Matthew know what you're doing. We don't want this house on our books again."

Raina blinked. She knew their house was a bank foreclosure, but she hadn't paid much attention to the previous owner when filling out the stack of paperwork. "Gold Springs Community Bank used to own my house? What happened to the previous owner?"

Chase's stern expression didn't change. "I can't disclose any information about the house without an order from a judge." His tone was clipped. He wasn't giving any information away unless necessary.

Raina could pretty much guess what happened. A bank wasn't in the business to purchase houses as investments. Either the previous owners failed to pay their mortgage, or they didn't complete the terms of their construction loan. She grimaced inwardly. The previous owners' situation was too close to home for comfort.

6

A LOVELY EXPLOSION

Once outside the bank, Raina strode over to City Hall while checking the voicemail left by her grandmother.

"Hi, Rainy. I blew up the microfiche machine. It couldn't keep up with the speed I was winding forward. I blamed it on the age of the machine, and the librarian believed me. Heh heh. I'm off to the newspaper office to see if they have any archives."

Raina chuckled as she deleted the message. Trust her grandma to make a mess out of a simple task. She probably considered it below her pay grade to spend the afternoon cooped up at the library. Her grandma didn't have the patience for research. She was a woman of action.

Her eyes widened as she recalled something about the message. Her grandma couldn't talk to Phil Lutz, the newspaper owner and editor, by herself. They took an instant dislike to each other when her grandma accused him of manipulating the public sentiment over the last election for the mayor.

Raina ground her teeth. If the newspaper office was their best option for finding archived information, she couldn't let her grandma light the bridge on fire, not after what she did at the library on her own. Raina would have to come back to the building permit office later. She spun on her heels and stepped off the sidewalk.

An angry horn blared next to Raina's ear. Tires squealed.

Someone grabbed Raina's arm and jerked her backward.

As she stumbled over the curb on the sidewalk, a lifted truck with dirty mud flaps rumbled passed. The driver screamed out the window. "Watch where you're going, idiot."

Raina righted herself and turned to thank her rescuer. All she saw was the back of a tall man trotting into City Hall. "Thank you," she hollered.

The man raised a hand in acknowledgment and disappeared into the building.

Raina took a deep breath, glad her grandma wasn't around to see her idiotic behavior. Getting herself killed wouldn't help the situation. They were counting on her to save the house.

Raina walked back to the bank and hopped in her car. The newspaper office was within walking distance, but she didn't want to give Po Po more alone time than necessary with Phil. If her grandma backed Phil into a corner, the newspaper owner would refuse to help them.

She got to the newspaper office lickety-split and jogged up the pathway to the main entrance of the single-story brick-front building. She trotted through the glass lobby door. The newspaper shared the premises with a title company and insurance company. The rent from these two businesses was probably what kept the weekly newspaper afloat.

Raina hooked a left at the fork, passed the restrooms, and opened the door to the newspaper office. A counter separated her from the main room. Three desks were pushed against one wall and two large flat screen TVs hung on the opposite wall. A door at the far wall opened to the editor-in-chief's office. The commercial printers for the newspaper itself were probably located in the rear of the building to muffle the noise from the machines. The newsroom was empty.

"Hello? Phil, are you here?" Raina called out. She didn't feel comfortable walking around the long counter that separated the makeshift waiting area from the newsroom. She hoped the lack of people wasn't from her grandma hiding Phil's body in the printer room out back.

"I'll be there in a minute," Phil called out, his voice muffled.

Raina frowned. His voice didn't sound like it came from the office, so he had to be somewhere in the newsroom. But with an open floor plan where there were only three desks and the wall-mounted TV monitors, she couldn't see where he could be.

A second later, Phil emerged from underneath his desk. Using the corner of the desk for support, he slowly pulled himself to his feet. The newspaper owner was close to sixty-eight years old. He had grumbled about retirement on and off for the last several years. He was the third generation in his family to run this weekly rag, and like his grandfather and father, he had another source of income to make this passion project financially viable. None of his grown children had shown any interest in taking over the newspaper, and maybe that was why he was still working.

Phil was once a tall man in his youth, over six feet tall. However, decades of using a typewriter—and later a computer—had given him a permanent hunch around his shoulders and a curve in his spine. His potbelly didn't help the situation either. His white hair was fluffy and wispy. He shuffled over to the counter and sat down at the barstool.

"Hi, Phil. What are you doing down there? Anything I can help with?" Raina asked.

"Loose cable," Phil said. "No big deal. It's getting down and up that's the problem. Only another year or so. Then I'm selling. What can I help you with, Raina?"

Raina breathed a sigh of relief. She had gotten here before her grandma. Better to skip the chitchat and get down to business even though she wanted to ask if there was a potential buyer. After all, the newspaper business was a dying industry. But she wouldn't want

Po Po interrupting them and Phil clamming up in her grandma's presence.

"I'm interested in articles from twenty to thirty years ago," Raina said.

Phil gestured at a bank of filing cabinets along the entire wall on Raina's right-hand side. "See those cabinets there?" At Raina's nod, he continued, "That's every article ever written in the *Gold Springs Weekly*. It goes as far back as my granddad's time. You'll have to be more specific."

Raina's jaw dropped. It would take days to rifle through all the files. "They're not digitized in a searchable database?"

Phil chuckled, his hand resting on his jiggling belly. "Ain't nobody going to look at those files but me, and I know where everything is. So why spend the money to have a computer guru set up a database I probably wouldn't use."

"I'm interested in articles about missing people," Raina said. If Phil had a filing system, maybe it wouldn't be as challenging to find the articles. She frowned. She had no idea if the remains were male or female. For all she knew, the remains could belong to a child. She shivered at the thought. Maybe she should wait until she got more information from the police first.

Phil leaned his elbows on the countertop. "This wouldn't have anything to do with the bag of bones found at your house yesterday, would it?"

Raina blinked. How did the news spread so fast? "How did you find out?"

"Someone saw the coroner van outside your house."

"Will this make it to the news this weekend?" Raina asked.

She didn't think there would be a chance that Phil would leave the story out. It was too juicy. With rumors already spreading like wildfire, everyone would pick up the edition just to see if there was more information. This, in turn, would sell more ad space.

Phil shrugged. "Sorry, my ace reporter is keen on printing it, and I have to agree with his assessment. People would want to know more details." He pulled a notepad and pencil from underneath the counter. "How about an interview?"

Raina shook her head. "You know I can't talk about an active investigation." Detective Sokol hadn't said she couldn't talk to anyone, but if she spilled the beans, it wouldn't take a rocket scientist to figure out who squealed to the press.

Phil opened his mouth—

A blast of cold air swirled in from behind Raina.

"Hello! Who started the party without me?" Po Po said.

Raina spun around to see her grandma step into the building. A few steps later, and Po Po stood next to Raina. Po Po gave Phil a chin tip in greeting, similar to how gangsters greeted one another as a sign of wary respect.

"Phil was just telling me how he found out about the remains," Raina said. She prayed her grandma would become a silent observer for the rest of the conversation.

Po Po fluttered a hand languidly as if giving Raina permission to continue. It took all of Raina's willpower not to roll her eyes. Her grandma could be a drama queen when the mood suited her. Raina's Tai Ma, Po Po's mother, had been an opera singer before her marriage. Acting was in their blood, according to Po Po. But more likely, it was an excuse for her grandma to do whatever she felt like doing.

Phil rolled his eyes. He had no qualms about showing his feelings toward Po Po's antics. "You and Matthew don't seem to be the type to go around murdering someone." He tapped the side of his head. "So if you put this together with the coroner van and the construction, you probably found an old murder victim. Am I right?"

Raina nodded. The newspaper owner was one sharp cookie. If he was able to make this connection, wouldn't someone else? Like the real murderer? She brushed the thought aside. She was probably reading too much into his comment. The murderer might have thought he or she got away with this killing years ago. Raina didn't want the murderer to believe she was on the right trail when she'd barely even made it out of the starting gate.

"Can you help me find those articles, Phil?" Raina

asked. She gave him her most charming smile. She had to stop herself from fluttering her lashes at him.

Phil flicked a glance at Po Po, and his expression turned grim. "It will take days to pull three decades of articles on missing people. And right now, I don't have the time."

"Do you have a filing system? If you teach me, I can look for it myself," Raina asked. She put her hands together in front of her and pleaded with her eyes.

"Raina, I like you, but I won't let you have free rein on my business. Unless you come back with a search warrant, I am not looking for those articles," Phil said.

"Can we file a public records request?" Po Po asked.

Phil gave her a deadpan stare. "The newspaper is privately owned by me. Your request for public information does not apply here."

Raina closed her eyes and rubbed her temples. Phil wouldn't yield to anything with her grandma here. Their dislike of each other made it pretty much impossible for him to concede to anything. She would have to come back another time without her grandma to try again.

"Now look here, Phil," Po Po said. "You can't withhold information from us. That's like aiding and abetting the murderer. You could be charged as an accessory."

Phil raised an eyebrow. His expression clearly said her grandma was a whack-a-do. "There's something called evidence in this country."

Po Po bristled at the dismissive tone. She rose to

her full five feet and placed her hands on her hips as if ready for battle. She opened her mouth—

"Thanks for your time," Raina cut in, grabbing her grandma's forearm and dragging her out the front door. "I'll give you that interview later."

Once next to Raina's car, she let go of her grandma's arm and unlocked the car. They got in.

"What are you doing?" Raina asked. "He won't tell us anything if you keep antagonizing him."

"Is that what I'm doing? I thought you're the good cop, and I'm the bad cop. Geez, Rainy, we got to get our act together before our next interview," Po Po said. "People will think we're amateurs."

Raina snorted and pulled onto the road. "We are amateurs."

"Practice makes perfect. What's next, Sherlock?"

"Can you call Iris Wells to see if she can meet us for coffee?"

"Your former real estate agent?"

"Yes, she might have information about the previous owner of the house," Raina said.

Po Po made the call while Raina drove to the senior center. Time to check in with Maggie and Frank to see if they made any headway with the senior citizens of the town. Hopefully, they would have better luck without her grandma's assistance.

7

THROWING DOWN THE GAUNTLET

The Posse Club gathered at the corner of the recreation room in the senior center. The room was the senior center's all-purpose room, and it reminded Raina of a school gymnasium. One set of double doors opened into the lobby of the senior center, where there was a communal kitchen, a quiet room for reading, and the office. Another set of double doors opened to the community garden and the parking lot.

Several groups of senior citizens played card games, board games, or puzzles on plastic foldable tables. The four of them looked conspicuous with their heads together, whispering for all its worth. The other senior citizens in the room watched them from the corner of their eyes. The club members—especially Po Po—were enjoying their moment of self-importance.

Po Po told them about the microfiche machine explosion at the public library. "And when I got to the newspaper office, Raina was already there grilling Phil. Did you get any information out of him?"

Raina shook her head. "Not a thing." She couldn't quite hide the exasperation in her voice. She dug out the little notepad in her purse.

Maggie raised an inquiring eyebrow at Raina. Her grandma's best friend could probably guess what had caused Phil to clam up. "We've got something to report," she said, leaning forward.

The scent of vanilla and cinnamon drifted over. Raina took a deep breath. She had learned to bake from her grandma-in-law's kitchen as a child. Even though Maggie didn't bake as much once her vision started to go south, she still smelled of warmth and comfort.

Frank sat back on his chair and crossed his muscular arms, sprinkled with fluffs of white hair. He still looked fit enough to be intimidating. Must be the former military bearing and training. Often Raina would see him when she passed the gym during her morning run.

As Maggie began her recital, Frank gave her a beaming smile, his teeth white against his dark brown skin. Though the two were newlyweds, they had been friends for many years, and the affection ran deep.

"There are three possible victims," Maggie said.

"Whoa! How do you know they could be victims?" Raina said, her pen hovering over her little notebook.

"She meant we found three missing locals in the last thirty years," Frank said. "There were others, but they were found later, usually hiding from their families."

Maggie nodded her thanks. "Yes, three missing people. There is Amber Dews. She was a welder down at the old steel plant. She was in her forties at the time of her disappearance nine years ago."

"I didn't know we had a steel plant in town," Po Po said.

"It closed down shortly after Amber's disappearance," Frank said, "though it had nothing to do with her. Just those jobs going overseas. The old building is still there in the industrial area."

"It's possible a steel welder could have worked on the house. Maybe she did some welding on the side to pick up extra money," Po Po said.

Raina frowned. "But it's unlikely. The house has always been two stories. So the previous owners wouldn't have needed someone like Amber to weld the steel beams to raise the structure."

"And then there is Sharon Mota," Maggie said. "She was about twenty when she disappeared about sixteen years ago. One of the college kids. She was known to be a party girl. So there was speculation that she went home with somebody after a party and never came back. Her poor parents stayed in town for months, demanding the mayor and the police to do something, but there weren't any leads."

"I don't see how Sharon ended up at the house," Po Po said. "Do kids go to construction sites to make out? She must have buns of steel to not get a rash from the sawdust and nails on the floor. That must be worse than sand in your butt crack."

Frank and Maggie glanced at each other and shared a smile. They were used to Po Po's off the wall comments.

Raina rubbed her temples. She didn't like appearing like a stick in the mud in front of the Posse Club, but she didn't want to think about other people's cracks either. Yuck. "I guess it depends on the timing. We need to know when the building permits were last pulled and if the house was vacant at the time of her disappearance." She made a note to check on the building permits for the house.

"So you're assuming the killer didn't open his wall and hide the body in it?" Po Po asked.

"A decomposing body isn't something you want to smell first thing in the morning," Frank said. "Even Folgers can't hide that aroma."

Raina nodded at Frank. "His point exactly."

"And there is Miles Lutz," Maggie said. "He was in his mid-twenties at the time of his disappearance."

"Lutz? As in a relative of Phil Lutz, the newspaper owner?" Raina asked.

Maggie nodded. "His younger brother."

Po Po pounded the table with her open palm, causing several people to gawk at them. "We got our victim and our killer."

"Shhh!" Raina hushed, putting her index finger to her lips. "Do we want to advertise what we're doing here? The more people who know that we're investigating, the more attention we'll get."

Maggie and Frank nodded gravely.

Po Po's eyes gleamed at the thought. "We could be famous."

"No. We could be dead," Raina said. "The murderer has gotten away with the crime for decades. Do you think the killer is going down without a fight?"

Po Po harrumphed and crossed her arms. "Oookay. I'll behave."

The corner of Frank's mouth twitched, and Raina averted her gaze to keep from laughing.

"Now, where were we?" Maggie asked.

Po Po partially covered her mouth with her hand and whispered with exaggeration, "We're at the part where I cracked the case. Phil killed his brother and hid his body in Raina's house."

"Let me guess. Phil's motive is to inherit the family newspaper," Raina said.

"Bingo! We've already solved the case," Po Po said, snapping her fingers and shimmying from side to side. "At this rate, we could be the next ghost whisperer."

Raina burst out laughing. Sometimes her grandma was just too much. By the time Raina wiped the tears from her eyes, Po Po was no longer preening.

"It looked like you had a brain fart, Sherlock," Po Po said with a hint of annoyance in her tone.

Raina didn't bother wiping the grin off her face. "I think we're getting ahead of ourselves. The newspaper isn't a money press. I don't think it's worth killing your baby brother to avoid splitting the inheritance."

"But don't forget about the family money," Frank said.

"True. But can you imagine Phil going into the office every day and being reminded of his baby brother's murder?" Raina asked.

Frank furrowed his brows. Unlike the rest of them, he had been born and raised in town. "I don't know. He's the Little League coach and donates money to a lot of charities. Unless all these good deeds are to make up for killing his brother..."

Raina raised an eyebrow. "Do you really believe it is all an act? It doesn't add up for me. No one can pretend to be a good guy for decades without something slipping."

Po Po swiveled her head between Raina and Frank as if following a tennis game. "Then how come he didn't mention his brother when you asked about missing local people?"

"Sometimes people don't want to talk about painful memories," Maggie said.

Raina had always been thankful to have Maggie to temper her grandma's more half-baked ideas. Though she usually went along with things, when she spoke, even her grandma recognized the voice of reason.

"Phil probably didn't want to get into a long-winded discussion with acquaintances," Raina said. Especially with her grandma hanging onto his every word. "And he might feel guilty about the disappearance."

"Guilty? How so?" As the child of the third wife in a polygamous marriage when it was still legal in China, Po Po didn't have much to do with her siblings and often saw them as rivals.

Raina nodded. "Yes, guilty. Phil is the elder brother. It was part of his unofficial job description to look out for Miles even when they were grown-ups. Maybe Phil thinks he failed his brother somehow. The newspaper is more of a family tradition than a paycheck. I just don't see it as being the source for such a heinous crime."

Frank nodded. "I don't see Phil being a suspect either. You never heard about the Lutzes having money problems even when folks were losing their houses left and right. And this was before Phil inherited the newspaper."

"Fine. I guess I'm outvoted," Po Po said.

"I'll have another chat with Phil and bring up the subject of Miles. In the meantime, can you ask around about who previously owned my house? The bank must have foreclosed on somebody. I would like to have a chat with them if they are still in town," Raina said. "But let's try to be more discreet about our interests."

The Posse Club members nodded.

A commotion by the entryway caught Raina's attention. And she turned around to see Janice Tally making her way into the recreation room, pushing a walker with tennis balls on its legs. Next to her was an unfamiliar senior citizen Raina hadn't seen before. She must be new.

"Oh great. Here comes Smelly Tally," Po Po said.

"Po Po! You gotta stop calling her Smelly Tally. Someday it'll slip out and embarrass you," Raina said. She hated sounding like her mother, but sometimes her grandma said the most outlandish things.

"I can't help it. She has the little old lady smell," Po Po said.

Raina's lips twitched, and she had to press them into a thin line to keep from laughing. Janice Tally was only two years older than her grandma. "What's the little old lady smell?"

"Mothballs and rose-scented paper." Po Po made a face. "It reminds me of my grandmother."

Raina burst out laughing again. She turned her head back to the entrance. Janice and her buddy were making their way over to the Posse Club's table.

Janice was a bird of a woman with big round glasses and a mean little walker. She had no fear of rolling on toes and stabbing people's backside with the knitting needles she kept in a pouch on the walker. While Janice had both hands on the walker, she moved with ease through the crowd like she was pushing a shopping cart through the supermarket aisles. Po Po had always claimed the walker was more of a prop than a necessity.

Raina frowned. Why was Janice coming this way? What did Po Po do this time to warrant a visit?

"Janice Tally coming this way," Frank whispered to Maggie, who was squinting because of the distance.

Maggie stood. "Frank, honey, we have to check on Poe. It's time to take him for a walk." Poe was Maggie's service dog. He used to be Maggie's shadow, but these days he got longer breaks from his duty with Frank in the picture.

Frank grabbed his wife's hand, and they left without another word.

As Raina watched the couple retreat from the recreation room, she couldn't help but wonder if maybe she should do the same. But her grandma wasn't someone who backed away from an oncoming confrontation with her arch-nemesis, which meant Raina would have to stay to offer her moral support.

Her cell phone dinged with an incoming message. She pulled it out of her purse and checked the text. It was from Iris West.

I will be at the Venus Café for the next hour doing some work.
Come by if you want to chat. I only have a few minutes.

This would give Raina the perfect excuse to high-tail it out of here if things heated up. When she glanced up, Janice Tally and her new buddy stood in front of them.

Janice opened her mouth—

"Hi, Janice. Who's the new girl?" Po Po asked, shifting her gaze to the other woman.

The new girl, as her grandma called the senior citizen, towered over all three of them, close to five foot ten. She had to be in her late sixties but was trim like she exercised regularly. Her hair was completely silver, and the bangs fell over her sharp blue eyes.

Janice hesitated as if mentally debating on whether or not to ignore Po Po's question. Senior citizens could be just as bad as toddlers when it came to sharing their friends. "Bucky, this is Bonnie Wong."

Raina perked up at the emphasis on her grandma's name. Was Janice spreading tales about Po Po already? She gave her grandma a sideways glance.

Po Po narrowed her eyes at her arch-nemesis.

Janice ignored the look. "Bonnie, she is Grace Brown. We call her Bucky. Her husband was the former mayor who saved our town back in the early nineties."

Po Po straightened in her seat. "Now, don't you go spreading rumors about me. We wouldn't want to give the new girl the wrong impression." There was a slight edge to her voice.

Raina sank back into her chair, hoping to blend in with the furniture. Yikes, the claws were out already. This was even worse than a bad episode of the mean girls in high school.

"I don't need to spread any rumors about you, Bonnie. Your misconduct speaks for itself. How many senior citizens do you know who get banned from participating in our field trips?" Janice asked, holding up one finger. "Just you."

"I didn't protest the judgment because it would cause dissent among our friends. Now let's not turn this into a Team Janice or Team Bonnie type of situation." Po Po smiled at Bucky and stuck out her hand. "I'm pleased to meet you."

Bucky gave Janice a sideways glance. She hesitated for a fraction of a second and shook Po Po's hand. "Yes, nice to meet you." Her tone was soft and demure. The perfect lady in an awkward social situation.

"Are you a dues-paying member at the senior center? Did you get a place in the complex?" Po Po asked.

Raina did a double take at her grandma's eager tone. Why did she care if the new girl got a unit at the senior condo complex? Her grandma was up to something.

Bucky snuck another glance at Janice. "I'm staying with my sisters until I figure out what I want to do. My husband just passed away after a lengthy illness, and I'm trying to figure things out."

Po Po's eyes softened. "My husband hung on for a year after his diagnosis. I went crazy for a bit. I don't remember much about it. Every morning was like a thick fog. It's probably best that you don't do anything for a while."

Bucky nodded.

"Come on, Bucky. Let me introduce you to the

regular folks," Janice said. She turned her back on them and went toward the group playing bridge.

Po Po ground her teeth. "Isn't it libel for her to spread tales about me? She's already trying to assassinate my character."

"Libel only applies to written text like the newspaper," Raina said, hoping she didn't sound too much like a Miss Know It All. "Why do you care what Janice thinks?"

During high school, her grandma had given Raina the advice to ignore the people who didn't appreciate her for who she was. They had no bearing on the important things in her life. Had her grandma forgotten her own sage advice?

"The vote for the social committee chair is coming up next month. I am going to dethrone Smelly Tally," Po Po said. There was a wicked gleam in her eye.

Raina's eyes widened. Yikes! Not only would there be skirmishes between Po Po and her arch-nemesis from now until the vote, but there could also potentially be a change in the leadership at the senior center. She better get her popcorn ready for the rubbernecking that was bound to happen.

"Were you trying to get Bucky's vote?" she asked.

"You've got it. Every vote counts, especially since most people don't vote. How do you think Janice got the spot for the last few years? It wasn't for her winning personality. She won by a landslide vote of twelve to five," Po Po said.

"You're right. That's not that many votes at all," Raina said.

"From the Posse Club alone, I've already got seven votes. Well, I would get all seven votes if they were in town to vote. I don't understand why senior citizens want to spend half the year in their second home," Po Po said.

Raina gave her grandma a deadpan look. Talk about the kettle calling the stove black. Her grandma also owned a house in San Francisco and frequently traveled to stay there throughout the year. "Let me know if you need anything from me. I have to go. I'm meeting Iris at the Venus Café."

She ignored a twinge of guilt for not inviting her grandma to come along. She didn't want the interview to go sideways like it did with Phil, especially since they had no leads on the case. No wait. The victim could potentially be Phil's younger brother, but this information was also found without her grandma's assistance. Maybe her Watson would have to sit this case out.

8

A SILENT CRY FOR HELP

Iris Wells was already sitting at a booth when Raina walked into the Venus Café. The real estate agent was speaking into her Bluetooth headset with her day planner laid out in front of her on the table. Even from a distance, Raina could tell the real estate agent was in the middle of making an appointment.

Raina waved to Iris, who acknowledged the greeting with an index finger. Raina nodded and gestured at the counter. She walked over and ordered her iced caramel macchiato and lingered by the pastry display until Iris finished her call. Even before the real estate agent took off her headset, Raina was sliding into the seat across from her.

"Raina, how are you? How's the new house?" Iris said.

Once again, Iris wore a white pants suit that

showed off her slim figure and height. Raina had to swallow her height envy. Even up close, she couldn't tell Iris's age. The real estate agent could be in her thirties or fifties. Not only was Iris in shape, but her smooth ebony skin hid all age spots and freckles. The only telltale sign she was mature enough to buy alcohol were the crinkles at the corners of her eyes when she smiled, which only added to her charm.

Raina hesitated. She didn't want to go into a song and a dance about her house remodel woes, but the real estate agent needed context if she was to provide information. "Have you heard the rumor?"

Iris reached for her coffee cup, taking a long sip as if to buy herself more time. "Yeah, but I'm not sure how I can help you. You have owned the house for close to a year, so it would be near impossible to undo the deal. And the bank did disclose everything to you at the time of the sale, so there isn't much we can do..." Her voice trailed off, and she gave Raina an apologetic crooked smile.

"Just so we're clear. We're not trying to get rid of the house. It's our dream house, even with all of its... quirks," Raina said. Fatal flaws would probably have been the appropriate word choice, but they were in too far for it to make a difference now.

Iris straightened in relief. "That's good to hear. When I got your grandma's call, it sounded like you want to take the bank to court. It would be expensive, and you might not win."

Raina sighed inwardly. Trust her grandma to

jumble up the message. "Nothing of that nature. I was hoping you could give me the name of the previous owner."

"You mean the people who owned it before the bank?" Iris asked.

Raina nodded.

"That information wasn't in any of the paperwork. Why do you want to find out who previously owned the house?" Iris asked.

The real estate agent didn't sound enthusiastic about the favor. And Raina didn't blame her one bit. Iris only got paid after the sale of a house. But Raina was counting on Iris's business acumen to kick in. After all, most people buy and sell at least a few homes in their lifetimes, and happy clients made recommendations to friends and family.

"The previous owners might know something about the remains hidden in the wall of my house. If nothing else, they might have seen or heard something that has to do with the murder," Raina said.

Iris's eyes widened. "Murder?" she whispered. "What...what makes you think this has anything to do with the previous owners?"

"I didn't say it did. I just want to talk to the previous owners. That's all."

"But what makes you so sure there was a murder?"

"How else do you think the remains got inside the walls? A person couldn't have accidentally fallen in."

Iris grimaced. "I see your point. How old are the

bones? Maybe it was already there before the previous owners had possession of the house?"

"Just from the glimpse I had, I'd say they are probably between ten to thirty years old."

Iris's hand tightened on the coffee cup, popping the plastic top off. She removed her hand and placed it on her lap, ignoring the cup. "I can ask the selling agent, but I don't think she will disclose the information because it wasn't relevant to the sale. Or she might not know."

Raina gave her a pleading look. "That would be fantastic."

Iris sighed. "I'll make one phone call, but that's all I'm willing to do to help. In my line of business, time is money. I can't afford to spend time on this."

Raina flicked a glance at the Bluetooth headset.

"You're not expecting me to make the call now?" Iris asked in surprise.

"No time like the present." Raina gave her an encouraging smile.

"I'm in the middle of something. When I have time, I'll make the call and get back to you," Iris said, pointedly glancing at her watch.

Raina reluctantly got up from the booth. There was no point in pressing the real estate agent. While Iris had made a good commission off of the sale of the house, she had also spent an enormous amount of time showing the Louies more than two dozen homes. "I appreciate your time. Thanks for helping me."

As Raina thought over their conversation in the

short drive home, she couldn't help but wonder why Iris had been especially upset when Raina discovered the potential age of the remains. After all, the victim was hidden in the house long before Iris came into the picture.

As USUAL, Raina got home before Matthew did. Her once cozy one-bedroom apartment felt like a toddler's shoebox, even though they had the majority of their stuff in a storage unit. At first, it didn't seem too bad because she figured this living arrangement would only last a few months. Now with the discovery of skeletal remains, they would be lucky to move in before the end of the year. This was not an auspicious start to their marriage.

After she put the steaks on the George Foreman grill, she chopped zucchini with more force than necessary. Her thoughts drifted to their situation. She was a piler. She liked to make little molehills in her living space, but as a former Marine, Matthew's eyes twitched around her piles. She wasn't sure why she developed this habit, but it had been a part of her identity since college. Now with her husband in the apartment, she felt this unspoken pressure to clean up.

The house had been the solution to her problem. She had counted on moving in and spreading out her piles to relieve the pressure. As the zucchini with olive oil and thyme roasted in the oven, she picked up the pile of mail and sorted it. Usually she would have been happier to let it pile up for another day or two.

And to top it off, she wasn't contributing much financially toward their household. While she was busy with her two part-time jobs and shuttling the two grandmas around, she wondered if Matthew thought she wasn't earning her keep. This was probably an absurd thought, but it formed in her mind, and she couldn't shake it.

Matthew came home just as she was setting the plates on the Goodwill dining table. The oak legs were banged up, but she liked to think a family with children had put the table to good use before trading up.

"You're home early," Raina said. "How was your day?"

He dropped his messenger bag on the plushy hand-me-down olive green sofa from Raina's sister. "It's not over yet. I'm just taking a break. I have to get back to the station in an hour and a half."

Raina sighed inwardly. She had learned that being a small-town cop wasn't a nine to five job. It was far cheaper for them to rely on overtime than to hire more staff because of the benefits. At least the extra money would come in handy. "Ready to eat?"

Matthew kissed her cheek and stepped around her to go into the galley kitchen to wash his hands. Raina dished out the food. For the next few minutes, they concentrated on eating.

When it looked as if Matthew had eaten enough to

take the edge off his hunger, she asked, "Have you heard from the coroner's office yet?"

He averted his gaze and made a noncommittal murmur.

She studied him for a long moment. Seriously? With their finances on the line, she thought he would follow the case closely even if he wasn't the lead detective.

"I found the name of the victim," she said with nonchalance.

He continued eating but gestured for her to go on.

Raina swallowed her rising annoyance. She couldn't tell if he was patronizing her or humoring her. Either way, she didn't like it. What happened to his confidence in her ability to help solve this case?

She told him what she had learned at the senior center, leaving out the source of her information. "So the victim is likely Miles Lutz, Phil's younger brother. He was in his twenties at the time of his disappearance."

Matthew choked, spitting out a lump of half-chewed steak.

She leaned back, barely avoiding getting hit on the face. Yuck. Next time she would have to time her comments to when her husband had no food in his mouth.

Matthew grabbed his diet coke and took several long swallows. When he was no longer hacking, he whispered hoarsely, "How did you find this out?"

Raina pointed an index finger at him. "Aha! You have heard from the coroner's office."

She glared at him. They were supposed to be on the same team, and yet he was withholding vital information from her. How was she supposed to investigate this without his help? He was her police link.

Matthew took a sip of water and wiped his face. He threw his napkin on the table. "I don't know how you do this. How is your intuition so accurate?"

Raina tried not to preen. After all, she didn't have much to do with finding the identity of the victim. But she did like surprising her husband. Her scattershot approach to an investigation was too much for his methodical brain.

She shrugged and gave him a modest look. "Did you find out anything else about the victim?"

"I really don't have any information, Rainy," Matthew said. "The only reason I even know this much was because Joanna and Youri were discussing the case by my desk. They didn't put any effort into lowering their voices."

"Could they have done this on purpose?"

"I don't understand what you're trying to say?"

Raina sighed. Talk about a lack of imagination. "Maybe the conversation was staged so you could overhear the details. This is their silent cry for help."

Matthew snorted. "I think you're reading too much into it."

Raina made a mental note to stop by the police station after her morning shift at the Venus Cafe tomorrow. She'd thought things were crystal clear between her and Detective Sokol. But instead of calling her and squealing like a stuck pig when he got the report from the coroner's office today, she had to wheedle the information from her husband. This was unacceptable, especially when their previous partnership had only benefited him.

9

TICK TOCK

Raina skipped her run and made it to the Venus Cafe by four in the morning. Since the cafe opened at five thirty to compete with the Starbucks two block away, they had to start baking early. Of course, they could purchase the baked goods wholesale like Starbucks, but the profit margin was much higher to make them from scratch. And they were able to put specialty items on the menu, which gave them a leg up on the Starbucks drive-through.

Since the Sullivans had their baby girl, Raina had agreed to take three of the morning shifts so they could get some much-needed sleep. She didn't mind coming in this early because her shift was done after the breakfast rush. With Matthew working all hours of the day, she often was able to meet up with him for a late lunch. Without this flexibility in her schedule, they probably wouldn't see much of each other at all.

This morning, she made an extra dozen muffins—

six sweet and six savory—for the police station. While Raina intended to put the squeeze on Detective Sokol, it wouldn't hurt to show up with his favorite spinach and bacon muffin. She even made sure there was an apple cinnamon muffin for his wife. After all, with the right bait, she might catch more flies.

After Raina's shift, she went home to shower and change. It was still too early to stop by the police station. Most folks would still be on their lunch break and not hungry enough to appreciate the goodies. Better to wait until closer to three o' clock when the staff was in the middle of doing paperwork. The massive paper trail to convict a criminal was staggering. It was a wonder anyone ended up in prison.

She got into her car and drove the one mile to City Hall. Normally she would have walked or biked, but she didn't want to hold onto the pastry box while traipsing all over town. The police station was another mile further, on the opposite side of the downtown area.

Raina opened the main door to City Hall and jogged up the one flight of stairs to the second floor. She signed in at the building permit counter. There was only one contractor on the sign-in sheet ahead of her. She sat in a plastic chair to wait for her turn.

She had gotten to know the permit clerk over the last few months. Sometimes she showed up with a pastry and coffee whenever she had to pick up something for the house construction. Luckily, everything she brought over was less than ten dollars and wasn't considered a gift according to the town's policy on bribery. Food had a way of smoothing a path and opening doors that other gifts didn't. Food came from a place of caring.

When the clerk called Raina's name, she strode up to the counter. After exchanging greetings, Raina asked, "Can I get copies of the building permits for my house over the last thirty years?"

The clerk blinked. "I don't think anyone has ever requested this before. I don't know our procedure for this. Let me check with my boss, and I will get back to you." She glanced at the sign-in sheet to see who was next in line.

Raina didn't have time to wait a day or two for them to come up with a procedure. Government officials could be quite finicky at times. And they might say no in the name of security. "I want to make a public records request. Please give me the public records of all the building permits on my house for the last thirty years."

There! By invoking the California Public Records Act, the building department now legally had to turn over all their records on her house. It was a hassle, and some government agencies hated the extra work these requests generated, but they couldn't legally refuse.

The clerk pressed her lips into a fine line. "You'll have to put in a request with the city clerk. Downstairs and to the left. She will get your request up to us, and we will get you what you need."

The slight chill in the clerk's tone made Raina

realize she had made a tactical error. Instead of a friendly request, she had turned this into legal wrangling. Why did she use blunt force when honey could catch more bees? What was she thinking?

"Sorry for the extra work. I'm sure you heard the rumor about the bones in my house. I want to see what was done previously and if things were done to code," Raina said.

The frown disappeared from the clerk's face, and she appeared mollified. "Our inspectors would have made sure the work is done to code. Since this is a public records request, we have to go through all the files, including the hard copies in storage boxes off-site. But don't worry, we'll get you what information we have by the ten days' deadline per our policy."

Raina kicked herself mentally. The clerk would do her job, but she wouldn't be quick about it. "Can I withdraw my request? I haven't put it down in writing it."

The clerk gave Raina a tight smile. "Sorry. Per our policy, a request can be made verbally for those citizens who didn't know about the Public Records Act. Please fill out the form with the city clerk so we can get started." She crossed Raina's name off the sign-in list. "Mr. Lincoln Douglass."

As a tall man came up to the counter holding several rolls of plans, Raina backed away from the counter. She knew defeat when it smacked her in the face. Maybe her husband was right. They were too close to this case to trust their judgment.

As Raina strolled to her car, she mentally berated herself for using brute force when a little finesse and free pastries would have gotten her results faster.

Her cell phone rang, and she dug it out of her purse. She slid into the driver's seat and glanced at the caller ID. It was from Chase McKenna, the bank vice president. Her hand tightened around her phone. Could the day get any worse? Maybe she should let this call go to her voicemail. If this were good news, he would have sent her an email. A personal call meant he probably hadn't signed off on their loan extension yet.

Raina tapped on the screen to accept the call. She forced a smile into her voice. "Hi, Chase. How can I help you?" After her defeat at City Hall, she wasn't sure what to expect. If only their regular loan officer would return early from his European vacation.

Chase intimidated her in a way that his younger colleague didn't. She wasn't sure if it was his traditional banker look with the suit and tie or his no-nonsense demeanor, but she felt like a bug under a microscope whenever she had to interact with him. And when she factored in how he had them over a barrel, the interactions were bound to be uncomfortable.

"Everything seems to be in order in terms of paperwork. But before I can sign off on this, well, I've heard a rumor about your house."

Raina sighed inwardly, hearing a silent shoe drop.

Great. Phil hadn't run the newspaper article yet, so everything was speculation. Unless the banker called the police station, he had no proof their construction would not be delayed indefinitely.

Should she play dumb? But then Chase might bother Matthew instead. She didn't want her husband dealing with this on top of the overtime hours.

"What rumor?" she asked.

There was a long pause at the other end. Raina bit her lower lip to keep from filling it with her babbling. Her lawyer uncle had often used this trick on criminals and family members alike to get them to disclose information they might have otherwise kept private.

After another heartbeat, Chase asked, "Do you have time to stop by the bank today?"

Raina wanted to shout no. "Is this something we can resolve over the phone? I have an appointment this afternoon." Her statement wasn't technically a lie. Just because Detective Sokol didn't know she was looking for him didn't mean they didn't have an appointment.

Chase hesitated as if he didn't know how to proceed. And maybe he didn't. The average homeowner probably never encountered a situation like hers. Her ability to stumble on dead bodies was nothing short of ridiculous. Sometimes, her life was a sitcom with her grandma as the loveable sidekick.

"I'm not sure how to say this, so I'll say it. Will the discovery of a dead body at your house delay the remodel completion date?" He spat the words out like bullets hitting a metal trashcan. Ping. Ping.

Raina winced at the words. From the bank's perspective, if the rumors were true, the original construction loan was already a bad investment, and a loan extension would compound the effect. Until the authorities released the hold on construction, there was no time frame on when they could resume work again on the house. For all the banker knew, this standstill could be weeks, months, or even years.

"Technically it wasn't a dead body. It's skeletal remains. And I'll know more once I speak with the lead detective in charge of the case," Raina said. She winced at how tentative she sounded. A toddler had more confidence in expressing herself.

"Normally I would have no problem approving the extension. However, under this extraordinary situation, I'm not sure how to proceed. We don't want to have this house on our books again," Chase said.

Raina crossed her fingers. "I'm sure we can resume construction again by this weekend." She hoped her ancestors were listening to her prayers.

"What is your backup plan? Your house has to appraise for more than the construction loan to roll into a traditional mortgage."

"Our contractor is planning to bring in an extra crew. And if worse comes to worst, we can replace the damaged drywall in the living room and live without the open floor plan downstairs."

"Is this option still possible?" Chase sounded skeptical.

"Yes, it's doable. We'd only removed one drywall

panel when we discovered the remains. Everything else is still in place. It's just a matter of replacing this one panel, retexturing the wall, and painting it," Raina said. Even though it sounded simple enough, it would still be a hassle. But it was the quickest solution if they were to run out of time.

"Well, I'm glad you have a plan." Chase didn't sound entirely convinced. "When you hear from the police, let me know what they have to say. You'll probably need to plan on accelerating construction once you get the all-clear from the police."

"Does this mean you are approving a loan extension?" Raina asked. She held her breath like a child waiting for a treat from a parent.

"You have another month before your original loan runs out of time. Let's say we're on hold until we hear from the police. I don't want to be too hasty in approving anything," Chase said. His voice was crisp and professional. And there was no arguing with his logic.

After Raina hung up, she sat for a long moment with her head on the steering wheel. If they ran out of time and couldn't create an open floor plan by demolishing the walls in her living room and kitchen, it wouldn't be the end of the world.

They could remodel again later after they saved enough money to do it without taking out another loan. At least this was the theory, but once Raina and Matthew moved into the house and started a family, it probably wouldn't happen for decades. She would have to learn to live with what she got.

Would she have to live with the ugly avocado green appliances for decades too? She shuddered at the thought of using the fifty-year-old oven to cook the Thanksgiving turkey. She took a deep breath and started the car. Time enough to dwell on this later. Detective Sokol better have some answers for her.

10

THE BIG SQUEEZE

Raina was still agitated when she walked through the front door of the police station. A bench lined one wall in the waiting area behind her. The large bulletin board on her left filled the wall with wanted posters and lost and found information. No warm and fuzzy community flyers here. The police station was built decades ago when they still favored wood-lined wall panels. Even with new double-paned windows, the interior often looked dim and stuffy.

Donna greeted Raina, and her eyes lit up at the pastry box. The front desk clerk was a plump, pleasant brunette with flashing blue eyes. She didn't have a malicious bone in her body, but she loved to wag her tongue. Probably because she often spent the day alone at the front counter and office area.

If her boss knew how easily she spilled the beans,

they probably would put her in a dark, dingy corner by herself. She also happened to have a sweet tooth but not the baking skills to match it.

"Did you bring us goodies?" Donna asked.

Raina nodded and placed the box on the counter. Her timing was perfect. "Is Matthew here?"

Donna rubbed her hands together and flipped open the lid. Her eyes were glued to the contents of the box. "Not yet, hon." She pulled a small plate from underneath the counter.

Good, Raina thought. She didn't want her husband to interrupt her. "What about Detective Sokol?"

Donna waved over her shoulders. "He's in the yard, talking to the mechanic about a noise coming from his car." She selected an apple cinnamon muffin and placed it on the small plate.

"Enjoy the muffins," Raina said, walking toward the hallway with the side door that led to the corp yard.

As a citizen volunteer, she had badge access to most areas of the police station. The more secure areas like the weapons and evidence rooms and the holding cells were off-limits to her. The front desk clerk didn't even look up from her plate when Raina disappeared from the foyer. Being the unofficial pastry maker for the department definitely had its perks.

She opened the side door and stepped out into the tree-shaded courtyard. The picnic table and bench were empty. Beyond the courtyard was the police vehicle parking lot. At the far end of the lot, was the repair shop with its doors rolled up and the police cruiser suspended on the lift. However, there wasn't a single person in sight.

Raina made a left going around the dumpster to the concrete pad with a basketball hoop nailed to the side of the police building. Sometimes the guys shot hoops during their break. Bingo! Detective Sokol leaned against the building with one leg propped up, smoking a cigarette. He was staring at the sky as if seeking answers.

When Detective Sokol saw Raina, he threw the cigarette on the ground and stuffed his hands into his pockets. He didn't wave to acknowledge her but watched her steady progress toward him. His eyes narrowed, and his frown deepened.

Usually, he was the one who sought her out for information on a case. But this time, the power had shifted between them. Not only was she insisting on being part of the case, but she had also threatened to reveal his incompetence if he wouldn't help her.

And Raina wasn't sure how to handle the situation. She wasn't used to being the aggressive one. On top of this, how would this impact the detective's working relationship with her husband? Detective Sokol considered Matthew his biggest rival for the next promotion.

"Hey, I just want to check in with you to see if you found out anything since we last spoke," Raina said, flashing her pretty smile.

"I can't talk about an active investigation with a civilian," Detective Sokol said. His tone was remote and professionally polite.

Raina raised an eyebrow. He sounded like he was afraid someone would listen in on their conversation. She glanced around and even looked over her shoulder, but there wasn't anyone around. "When can we resume construction again?"

"The forensic team is combing the house and the grounds even as we speak. Hopefully, they'll get done by Saturday."

"I heard that the coroner's office has information about the remains."

"And where would you hear this information? Is it from your husband, Matthew Louie?" Only the glint in his eye gave away his keen interest in her answer.

"Of course not. Matthew would never discuss police business with me. I had to go about it the roundabout way by asking nosy questions," Raina said. Did he think she would be stupid enough to admit that her husband would tell her things about work? "Now, why are you acting all weird? I thought we were partnering up on this."

"Partnering up on what?"

"That we would try to resolve the situation at my house as quickly as possible," Raina snapped. She was at the end of her patience. With the bank questioning the viability of extending their loan, she didn't need this idiot making the situation worse.

"I don't know what you're talking about. I didn't make any deal with you."

Raina scowled at him and took a step closer. What was going on here? "I don't know what game you're playing, but you will not mess this up for us."

"Are you threatening me?"

"No, but your supervisor might find out about all those times you had help with your cases."

"So you are threatening to make trouble for me at work?"

"I don't have to make trouble for you. You do it to yourself. You don't know how to run an investigation properly."

"Are those words from Matthew?"

"No. Why are you so obsessed with my husband?"

"I'm not obsessed with him. I want to make sure he's not sabotaging my career."

Raina rolled her eyes. "The only one sabotaging your career is yourself. Now help me help you. I know the victim is Miles Lutz. He was in his late twenties at the time of his disappearance about thirty years ago. Now it's your turn. What do you have to share?"

Detective Sokol gave her a puzzled look. "How in the world did you learn this? Matthew has been talking to you."

Raina ignored the comment. "I see how it is. You plan to drag this investigation out until the bank forecloses on us. Without my help, your career is as good as dead."

"You need to stop harassing me. Just because your husband thinks he's a hotshot doesn't mean it's okay for you to bully me around."

Raina gaped at him. Harassing and bullying him? Those were inflammatory words. Where did he come up with this idea? "Sometimes I think you're an idiot."

Detective Sokol pulled his hand out of his pocket and held up his phone. He tapped on the screen to stop recording.

Raina gasped. Was this why he stuck his hands in his pocket as soon as he saw her? To record their conversation? What a jerk. "What do you think you're doing?"

"I'm getting you off my back. Don't make me turn this over to the deputy chief. I'm sure your husband would like to explain your behavior to his boss."

"You wouldn't dare."

Detective Sokol raised an eyebrow. "Don't tempt me."

Raina stared at him for a long moment. Had he only been waiting for an excuse to get her husband in trouble? "Why are you doing this? We've both benefited from our previous partnership. By pulling this stunt, I will never help you again."

He snorted. "I'm surprised you can get through a doorway with your swollen head. You are not the only clever woman in town."

Raina took a deep breath and almost choked at the rotting scent of the nearby dumpster. She couldn't believe she didn't smell it earlier, probably because she was too distracted by the conversation. "What are you planning to do with the recording?"

Detective Sokol stuffed his phone back into his pocket. He patted the bulge and said, "Nothing. It's nice to have an insurance policy."

"I see. I guess this means we're not working this case together."

"*Au contraire*. You're still working this case, and you'll tell me who you talk to you and what you found out."

"Wait a minute. You want me to solve this case for you?"

"And don't forget the red bow."

Raina blinked. How was this any different from their previous partnership? "But there are parts you have to do because you're the lead detective. And how can I solve this case if you do not share information with me?"

"Tough luck. Maybe you can ask your husband for the information."

Raina pressed the palms of her hands to her forehead. This circular logic was giving her a headache. The only thing that changed was Detective Sokol's insistence on involving Matthew in the case.

"Besides, it sounded like you already guessed most of it," he said. "We've gotten a sample from Phil Lutz to run a DNA test to see if we can get a match."

"Did the report mention how he died?"

"A blow to the head with a blunt object. Probably a hammer or something."

"Once we've positively identified the victim, what's the next step?" Raina asked. She didn't need a positive ID when her gut told her she was on the right trail and that Phil knew more than what he had let on.

"Before I do anything, I'm waiting for all the reports to come in."

"This could take weeks!"

Detective Sokol shrugged. "It's a cold case. Another week or two will not make much of a difference to the victim."

"But what about the construction on my house?"

"Then you should probably dig a little faster." There wasn't a hint of sympathy in his voice. He pushed himself away from the wall and strolled toward the repair shop.

Raina gaped at his back. Seriously? Did he say he wasn't investigating the case at all? And why did he record their conversation? To shift the power between the two of them, so he now had the upper hand? What a jerk.

She wanted to scream but settled for curling her hands into fists by her side. She kicked the basketball; it bounced off the wall and slammed into her shins. Ouch.

As Raina rubbed her leg, she ran through her conversation with Detective Sokol. What kind of sleuth let someone record her conversation? Hands in the pocket was the oldest trick in the book. She had used it several times herself. Amateur hour had more talent than she displayed today. What made her think she could run with the big boys? She couldn't even get the bank to approve a loan extension.

Before Raina could wrap her misery like a cloak around herself, her cell phone rang. She pulled it out of her purse. The call was from Po Po. She wasn't in the mood to talk to her grandma, but the call might distract her from the dark thoughts. Besides, she was already on strike two for the day, and she didn't think she should be left to wander around town unsupervised.

The last thing she needed was to get her husband fired from the police department. She cringed at the thought. Now, that would be her worst nightmare—a thousand times worse than losing the house.

"Hi, Po Po. Did you find out who previously owned my house?" Raina asked, strolling back into the building and heading for her car. Please let there be some good news.

"No. Something came up at the senior center, so both Maggie and Frank are off the case. It's just me and you, Sherlock," Po Po said.

"Did something happen with Smelly Tally?" Raina grimaced. "I mean Mrs. Tally."

Po Po burst out laughing. "I got you saying it." She laughed again, gleefully. "Now, if only I can get everyone else to call her this. People can't elect someone with a name like that to be the social committee chair."

Raina smiled. Trust her grandma to focus on the important stuff. "Po Po! You are so bad."

"Rainy, you got to come over to the dark side. It's a lot more fun when you can walk that fine line between respectable and vulgar. Usually, people settle for eccentric because they don't know what else to call you. It's your free pass to do and say whatever you want."

"You have to give me another two decades before I can get away with eccentric. Right now, I'll settle for being a good wife to a police detective."

"Suit yourself." Po Po's tone implied that Raina didn't know what she was missing. "I hope you're not rolling your eyes at me, young lady." And just like that, Raina's funky mood dissipated. She was still worried about the recording, but there was nothing she could do about it at the moment. Wasting mental energy on something that was beyond her control was useless.

"What are you doing later? Want to grab an early dinner? I have something for you," Po Po said.

Raina perked up at the thought of an unexpected gift. "When do you want me to pick you up? Matthew is working late again. He can always pick up a sandwich for dinner."

"Now that's my girl," Po Po said. "Let him fend for himself. How about an hour from now?"

Even through the phone line, Raina could tell her grandma was beaming at her. While she might be a grown woman, it felt good to bask in her grandma's approval, especially after her miscalculation with

Detective Sokol. She glanced at the clock on the dashboard of her car. "Perfect."

There was just enough time to swing by the newspaper office and put the squeeze on Phil. If the lead detective for the case wasn't willing to help her, she was more than capable of helping herself.

11

TAKING CARE OF OUR OWN

As Raina pulled into the newspaper office's parking lot, a chirping sound filled the air, followed by a vibration from inside Raina's purse. She parked and dug the phone out of her purse. The text message was from Iris West, the real estate agent.

THE SELLER AGENT DOESN'T HAVE THE INFO. SORRY.

Raina always knew it was a longshot. If the seller had the previous owners' information, it would have been much quicker than waiting for the public information request at the permit counter. She replied to the message, thanking Iris for her time.

She was about to put her phone away when it dinged again.

HAVE YOU HEARD FROM THE POLICE ON WHEN YOU

COULD RESUME CONSTRUCTION?

Raina studied the message for a moment. She was touched that Iris cared, especially since everyone she had dealt with today only wanted to know the status because it impacted their bottom line. Or maybe the real estate agent only wanted to know if Raina had thoughts of putting the house on the market?

She hated being so suspicious, but she was operating in the dark. She had no idea who were the good guys and the bad guys in a cold case with no leads. She replied to the message.

CONSTRUCTION IS ON HOLD INDEFINITELY. THE POLICE ARE SCOURING THE ENTIRE PROPERTY FOR CLUES.

It wouldn't hurt to spread the rumors that this case had top priority for the police department. It was time to see if Raina could smoke the killer out. And nothing would make this person more nervous than close police scrutiny.

Iris replied back to the text message.

OVER UNIDENTIFIED REMAINS?

Raina bit her lower lip. Should she show her hand? While Iris was not a suspect, she knew and spoke to a lot of people throughout the day. Raina replied back.

WHO SAID THE REMAINS ARE UNIDENTIFIED?

Iris immediately responded.

Who is it?

Raina replied.

Sorry. It's need to know.

Iris's texted back.

I'm surprised they have the manpower to devote this much attention to a cold case.

It was one thing to put pressure on, but another to spread outright lies. And yet, Raina was already in the fray, so she might as well keep swinging in the hopes of hitting something. She replied back to Iris's message.

You know how it is with the police fraternity. Matthew is one of their own. They take care of their people.

Raina waited for a couple of minutes, but there was no return message. Did she hit a nerve, or did Iris get distracted by something? It was hard to gauge what silence meant in a text conversation.

She strolled through the lobby of the building. From outside the entrance of the newspaper office and through the glass door, she saw Phil typing on a laptop at the front counter. She hated the thought of disturbing his intense work, but she needed answers. Unfortunately, his connection to the victim was the only lead she had on the case.

Since Phil willingly gave the police a sample of his DNA, he probably suspected his brother was the victim. But from his intense concentration, he probably hadn't heard the news from the police yet.

The appropriate thing to do would be to come back tomorrow. By then, the police would have contacted Phil about his brother's demise. That would be the right thing. If only she weren't so desperate.

As if on cue, Phil glanced up and met her eyes through the glass pane. He hesitated and nodded slowly in greeting. He tapped on his laptop and closed the screen. He folded his hands on the countertop and waited for her with eyes that seemed to expect the world to end.

With each step, Raina's body temperature rose. By the time she opened the door, a bead of sweat had rolled down the small of her back. She hated being the bearer of bad news.

They exchanged polite greetings and fell silent. Raina shifted from foot to foot. *Just tell him*, she told herself.

"I was expecting the police, but I guess with your husband working at the station, you're the next closest thing," Phil said. The tightness around the corner of his eyes betrayed his anxiety.

"Not even close. Matthew is not on this case. I'm just my normal nosy self. Also, until the police find out how the remains got inside our house, we can't even resume construction," Raina said.

"Have you heard anything? Do they..." Phil licked his lower lip. "Do they know who it is?"

Raina studied the newspaper owner. Was he only nervous because positive identification meant he would lose any hope of seeing his brother again? Or was he worried because he killed his brother? "It's Miles, your brother."

Phil turned ashen, and sweat popped up on his upper lip. His hands curled into fists near his heart. He closed his eyes and trembled.

Raina reached for his hands. They were cold and clammy. "Phil. Are you okay? Is it your heart?" She wasn't sure if he had heart problems, but she didn't want to be the person to give him a heart attack.

Phil shook his head but couldn't speak. A single tear ran down his face. "I need to sit down for a moment." His voice was brittle.

Raina ran around the front counter, grabbed his elbow, and led Phil to his office chair. She trotted to the water dispenser, grabbed a paper cup, and filled it. By the time she got back to Phil, he was still ashen, but he was no longer clutching his heart.

"Here's some water," Raina said, pressing the paper cup into Phil's hand. "I'm sorry. I thought you knew already." *Liar, liar*, said a small voice inside her head.

She had blurted out his brother's name to see how Phil would react. His reaction wasn't the look of someone who had gotten away with murder. It was the reaction of someone who had finally lost all hope. What happened all those years ago?

"I told Miles to leave it alone. I told him to walk away from it. But no, I could never tell him what to do. He just had to help the girl, and it got him killed," Phil mumbled to himself.

"What happened?" Raina whispered. Phil was talking as if going over an old argument. She was afraid to breathe. It might break the spell.

"Miles was working on a story. He said it would be big enough to get him on the map because a dirty politician was involved. But I don't think he was after the politician. He was trying to help the girl save her parents' house."

"Who's the girl? What's her name?" Raina leaned closer. This could be the break she had been waiting for.

Phil shook his head. "I don't know. It was someone he dated in high school. He changed girlfriends so often that I couldn't keep up with it. And we had a newborn at the time. I thought he had enough sense to deal with it."

"And she wanted help to save her family's home?" Raina asked. This must be the daughter of the previous homeowners for her house. "Why did she think Miles could help her?"

"My baby brother should have been Irish. He probably razzle-dazzled her with the important stories he had worked on as a reporter." His voice choked, and he closed his eyes as if to hide his emotions. "The fool."

After this initial burst of information, Phil clammed up. He was grieving for his younger brother, so Raina excused herself and left. When she got back to her car, she sat for a long moment, digesting what she had heard.

How much of Phil's grief stemmed from guilt for not stopping his younger brother from pursuing a dangerous story? Even though Miles was an adult, Phil probably couldn't help but feel responsible. After all, this was practically the job description of most firstborns.

Would the story expose the circumstances of the previous owners' foreclosure? Could this potentially be a fraudulent case against the Gold Spring Community Bank? Who was the banker responsible at the time? Either someone who had long since left the bank or had risen through the ranks. If this banker still lived in town, he or she might have a lot to lose if an old fraudulent case came out.

And last, who was Miles's high school sweetheart? This was probably easy enough to find out. The library had a copy of every single yearbook ever published by the high school.

Raina glanced at the clock on the dashboard of her car. The library was probably closed for the day, and it was time to meet her grandma for an early dinner. She started the car engine. As she pulled out of the parking lot, she felt almost cheerful at the turnaround to her day. At least she was back in the game again and not hitting dead ends.

12

DOUBLE ACE

Po Po was already waiting for Raina when she pulled up next to the curb in front of the senior condo complex. She wore a red velvet tuxedo jacket with black velour jogging pants and her white orthopedic sneakers.

When Po Po slid into the passenger seat, Raina said, "Nice outfit."

Her grandma beamed. "Thanks, it's my campaigning outfit. Janice and I had our first debate this afternoon. I thought a suit might be a little too stuffy. My entire platform is all about shaking things up. Down with the old system." She pumped her fist in the air to punctuate her words.

Raina averted her gaze so her grandma couldn't see her smile. Eccentric might not be a strong enough word to describe her grandma. Crazy might be a better choice. Crazily lovable. She pulled away from the curb and merged into traffic. "Where are we having dinner?"

"The Pancake House. We're meeting someone there."

"I hope you're not setting me up on a blind date again. I'm off the market now."

"Oh, my dear child, I hope you never have to use my matchmaking services again."

Raina snorted. "Yeah, you're pretty bad at matchmaking."

"That's not what I meant."

Raina knew exactly what her grandma meant. There had been only one divorce in her family, and she wasn't planning to be the second. She gave her grandma a cheeky grin. "So who won the debate?"

Po Po shrugged. "We got interrupted by the senior center director. The funds to the Napa wine tour grew legs."

Raina's eyes widened. "Didn't she lock it up in her safe or deposit the money into a bank account?"

"I have no idea. I'm still banned from field trips, so I don't pay attention to what happens to the money," Po Po said.

"How long is your ban? Hasn't it been over a year?"

"Yeah, but who's counting? As long as Smelly Tally is the social committee chair, she seems to find an excuse to extend my ban every month."

Raina raised an eyebrow. Her grandma probably organized a prank each week, but only got caught once a month. But this explained her grandma's sudden interest in ousting her arch-nemesis.

"By the way, Maggie and Frank are out," Po Po said.

Raina pulled into the parking lot for the Pancake House. "Out of what?"

"The murder investigation. They're busy tracking down the missing field trip money."

Hallelujah! As much as Raina loved having a team to help with the legwork in this cold case, she didn't want Maggie or Frank accidentally interacting with the murderer. They might end up on the killer's radar. It was bad enough having to worry about Po Po, but her grandma was a wily fox with plenty of tricks. And since she was a known eccentric in town, most people dismissed her as a harmless or crazy old lady, which meant she wasn't a threat to anyone. In some ways, her grandma's outlandish behavior was protection.

Raina and Po Po went inside the restaurant and slid into a green vinyl booth by the window where they could see out into the parking lot. The server gave them menus and a caddy full of candy-colored syrups.

"Who are we meeting?" Raina asked, flipping through the menu. Pancakes or waffles? It was a tough decision. The seasonal apple cinnamon butter sounded like a winner.

A teenager with shaggy black hair rolled up next to the window on his too-small bike. His bony knees stuck out on the sides like a clown in a circus ring. He locked up the bike and tapped on the glass to get their attention. Po Po gave him the thumbs-up sign.

He was of Middle Eastern descent and had grown since the last time Raina saw him, now standing at close to five foot eleven. His large brown eyes were mostly hidden underneath his shaggy hair. Fluffs of black hair dotted his upper lip like he was trying to grow a mustache but ended up with a science experiment.

As the teen strolled through the entrance and headed to their booth, Raina noticed he walked with a stoop like his head was too heavy for his toothpick neck. At least his long sleeve shirt was tucked into his baggy jeans like he attempted to appear presentable.

He slid into the booth next to Raina, giving her the once over and a cheeky grin. "S'up, babe. Do you remember me? It's T-Dawg."

Raina rolled her eyes. This again? He had given her information to locate a suspect in one of her previous investigations. "Oh, I remember you. My grandma vouched for you so you could join the Science Ninja Club. And I know for a fact that your name is not T anything."

The teen glanced at Raina from the corner of his eyes as if trying to figure out if he should keep up with the act. He glanced at her grandma, who was watching him like she was waiting for a train wreck. He returned his gaze to Raina. "It's Ahanu Ahmet."

"He's Double Ace," Po Po said. "That's his code name."

"I have a code name?" Ahanu asked.

"Of course. Everyone associated with me has code names." Po Po lowered her voice. "If the authorities catch us, we can't give them names because we don't know each other's real identity."

Ahanu leaned forward and nodded, drinking in every word. "That's real smart. What's your code name?"

Po Po pointed at herself. "I'm Watson." She pointed at Raina. "She's Sherlock."

Ahanu sat back with a frown on his face. "Um, aren't they old dudes from old books?"

Po Po stiffened. "They are the best detective team ever."

Raina burst out laughing. Oh, this was prime. She wiped the tears from her eyes. Her day was definitely turning around.

The server came by and took their orders. Raina ordered cinnamon apple waffles, and her grandma ordered a plain omelet the size of her face. She must be on a new diet plan. Normally her grandma would drown her pancakes in at least two flavors of syrup. Ahanu ordered two meals and a milkshake with extra whipped cream.

"Two meals?" Raina exclaimed.

Ahanu shrugged. "Why not? I love free food. Thanks, Po Po."

Raina glanced at her grandma. When did her grandma take another troubled teen under her wing?

Po Po stared placidly back at Raina. "Why not? I can't take the money with me when I'm dead."

Raina reached across the table and squeezed her grandma's hand. "Yes, why not? As long as it makes you happy."

Po Po leaned forward and patted Raina's cheek. "And this is why you're my favorite."

Ahanu's gaze shifted between the two women. "I'm lost. What just happened?"

The two women grinned at him.

"Grown-up stuff," Po Po said.

Ahanu straightened as if to protest, but Raina leaned forward, cutting him off. She glanced over her shoulder and whispered, "What's the weapon of mass destruction?"

Po Po tipped her head at Ahanu. Her grandma assumed the role of a more senior agent. "Your show, Double Ace."

Raina sipped her glass of water to hide her smile. Snickering at a moment like this would burst everyone's bubble. These two were like kids pretending to be spies in their imaginary world. Did her grandma even recognize the potential danger of helping Raina in these murder investigations?

Ahanu glanced around to make sure no one was watching them. No one even looked in their direction. He slid a thin metal card across the table toward Raina. It had a lot of notches and cutouts on it.

Raina glanced at it and back at Ahanu. "Is this one of those wallet tools? One of the gizmos that can replace a Swiss Army knife." She had given a wallet tool card to Matthew a while back, and it was now in the junk drawer.

"This is the new and improved version made for the master criminal," Ahanu said.

Po Po cleared her throat and widened her eyes at the teen.

Ahanu reddened. "I mean a master detective." He ran through a list of the card's attributes: lock pick, plastic zip tie cutter, a screwdriver, mini saw, bottle opener, and even a cell phone holder. What master criminal didn't have one of these on his Christmas wish list?

"It looks too thin to be able to cut through a plastic zip tie. Will it warp the first time I use it?" Raina asked, not bothering to keep the skepticism out of her voice.

Ahanu gave Raina an offended look. "Have a little faith, woman. The blade is coated with diamond dust, and the metal is titanium. And it costs Po Po a fair bit of money to get the raw materials to us. The Science Ninjas are not a bunch of hacks."

Raina raised her eyebrow at her grandma.

"There's nothing wrong with questioning authority figures," Po Po said.

When had Raina become an authority figure? Maybe her grandma was turning these troubled teens into criminal masterminds after all. She picked up the gizmo and dropped it in her purse. "Thank you for all your hard work. I'm sure this will come in handy."

There wasn't even a hint of sarcasm in her voice. These weapons of mass destruction her grandma had given her over the years had turned out to be useful at the oddest moments.

A tall, lanky teen with a backpack slung over one shoulder walked into the restaurant. He had light brown hair, turquoise blue eyes, and a familiar peanut-shaped face. Raina knew she had seen the kid before.

Ahanu stuck his upper torso off the side of the booth and waved at the teen, who jerked a thumb at a booth at the back of the restaurant. Ahanu nodded. He turned back to Po Po and Raina.

"Can you ask the server to bring my food over there?" Ahanu pointed out a general direction further down the restaurant. "There's a guy I know from school."

"Who's that? He looks familiar," Raina said.

"That's Forrest McKenna. He's the quarterback on the football team. The dude has problems with his math class. And he's paying me to tutor him." Ahanu wiggled his eyebrows. "And I'm not cheap."

"Sounds like an enterprising business," Po Po said.

Ahanu frowned. "I might stop after this exam."

"Why? Especially if he is paying top dollar," Raina said. Ahanu's mother was a single mom who left at the crack of dawn to clean houses. Their family could use the money.

Ahanu leaned forward and lowered his voice. "He drinks a little too much, and I think he has a drug problem."

"Marijuana?" Po Po asked.

Ahanu shook his head. "No, it's the prescription stuff. I think he got hooked on them when he injured his knee last year. Sometimes he can be a little volatile. He might need me to help him pass an exam, but he's not above picking on me when we're at school in front of his buddies. Nope, this money is too rich for my blood." Ahanu sounded glum.

Po Po nodded. "Sounds like you thought this through. It's probably a good idea. And if you need extra money, young man, I can always use somebody with a strong back. My friend is moving out of her unit, so we need help packing up. We're not spring chickens anymore."

Ahanu brightened. "Oh, yeah? I'm good with moving boxes."

"I can also use somebody's help with grocery shopping," Po Po said. "Lugging bags of groceries from the car to my condo, it gets tiring. Actually, the whole thing is tiring."

Raina gave her grandma a sharp look. Her grandma didn't grocery shop or cook. Raina did the grocery shopping for both of them and made the meals, delivering a hot meal a few times each week and several tubs for the freezer.

"Having someone do the grocery shopping would be a great idea," Raina said. "I'm always worried somebody will knock my grandma over at the grocery store. Give me your email address, and I will send you a list a couple of times a week. We'll pay for your time to do the shopping and the delivery."

Ahanu's eyes widened. "Really?"

Po Po nodded. "I'll ask around and see who else would want someone to do the shopping for them. A lot of the seniors need help with stuff like this. Maybe you can drive them to appointments."

Ahanu hung his head. "My car needs new tires. I don't want to put any more miles on them than necessary. I need to be able to drive my mom to work in the morning."

"You can drive their car. They're just too old to drive themselves," Po Po said. "Or you can use my car. It's probably not good for my car to sit in the parking lot most of the time."

Raina bit the inside of her lip to stop from giggling. How could anyone not love her grandma's generous heart?

"Thank you so much," Ahanu said. His voice cracked. As he slid out of the booth, he turned and hugged Po Po. He strode toward Forrest's booth with a skip in his step.

Po Po watched him disappear from their sight. "He's a good egg. Anyone who wakes up before school to drop his mom off at work has my support."

Raina stared after Ahanu's retreating back for a long moment. Didn't Chase McKenna have a son who played football? She ran through her interactions with the vice president of the bank. Forrest and Chase had the same last name. What were the odds that Forrest wasn't Chase's son?

Po Po waved a hand in front of Raina's eyes, breaking into her thoughts. "What are you thinking about? I thought I lost you there for a moment."

Raina met her grandma's eyes. "Chase McKenna has a son who plays football."

"Okay, but I don't get your point," Po Po said slowly. "Who is Chase?"

"Chase is the vice president of the Gold Springs Community Bank. He's holding my loan extension application hostage until the police say we can resume construction again. I wonder if he knows his son is addicted to prescription painkillers."

"What does this have to do with the murder investigation?"

"Maybe nothing. Maybe everything. It's just a tidbit of gossip that I might be able to use to throw him off my trail."

"I still don't get it."

Raina told her grandma about her conversation with Phil earlier. "If there is a fraudulent foreclosure case with the previous owners, the banker who closed the deal has either moved on to another job, retired, or might be a senior member of the bank."

Po Po nodded. "Like Chase McKenna."

"Exactly! He is either particularly careful about the deals he makes for the bank, or he just might be a little too interested in my house. It's worth keeping an eye on him all the same."

The server returned with their food. She didn't even blink when Po Po asked her to deliver Ahanu's food to a different booth. "You can put their tab on us."

For the next few moments, they ate in silence. As the food expanded in her stomach, Raina sighed with contentment. Everything would turn out okay. She would solve the case, and they would resume construction. Life was good.

"So what happened at the police station?" Po Po asked, breaking into Raina's thoughts.

Raina froze, her fork suspended in mid-air. A drop of syrup slid off the fork and dropped back onto her plate. She took a deep breath. It was time to confess her miscalculation.

13

DIE TRYING

The food sat like a lump of coal in Raina's stomach. Gosh, couldn't her grandma let the waffles digest first before asking uncomfortable questions? And how much should she tell her grandma who already didn't like Detective Sokol? Po Po could use the recording incident to launch an operation with the Posse Club to get back at him.

Raina didn't need another thing to add to her list of worries. Unlike the other people in town, Detective Sokol held grudges and had the authority as a law enforcement officer to make life difficult for the senior citizens. Even though it might be political suicide for him to do so, who knew if he had a logical side to rein him in.

She took a deep breath and told her grandma what happened with Detective Sokol and his little insurance policy. By the time she was done with her tale, she couldn't keep the frustration out of her voice any longer. "I should probably ignore his power display, but this nagging voice in the back of my head tells me that I can't trust him."

"Of course, you can't trust him. What if he uses this recording to blackmail you or Matthew?" Po Po said.

"No, he wouldn't do that."

"Do you really believe this?"

"I don't know what to do. Short of stealing his phone, breaking his passcode, and deleting the file, I don't think there's anything I can do about it."

"I could probably arrange that," Po Po said.

"Did you just say we can hack his cell phone?"

Po Po nodded. "Yes, I can arrange that."

Raina gaped at her grandma for a full heartbeat. "Are you sure you're not turning those kids in your Science Ninja Club into criminal masterminds? Po Po, I don't want to have to bail you out of jail someday."

Po Po rolled her eyes. "These kids are not doing anything illegal. And the person I have in mind to hack Detective Sokol's phone is a real-life hacker. The FBI hires him to do these security exercises on their computer system. So hacking a cell phone is probably a cakewalk for him."

"He sounds expensive."

"Don't worry about the cost. This guy owes me a favor, so I don't think it'll cost you anything."

Raina blinked again. Her grandma kept surprising her. What self-respecting hacker would owe a little old lady a favor? "Let me think about it. It feels wrong to break into his cell phone. It's probably uploaded to his cloud service, so just breaking into his phone is probably not good enough."

"But his phone is linked to his cloud service. If you hack his phone, you can hack into his cloud service. Trust me, Rainy, it can be arranged. I'm leaving this on the table in case you change your mind."

Raina shook head. The idea was so appealing but ethically wrong. If the hacking ever pointed back to her, Matthew's job was toast. She couldn't risk it. But boy, did it sound appealing.

AFTER DINNER, Raina went over to Po Po's condo to watch a movie. By the time Raina got home, Matthew was already getting ready for bed. She decided to join her husband, and there wasn't time for much talking after that. Since Raina didn't have a shift at the Venus Cafe the next morning, she slept in. When she got up, Matthew was already gone for the day.

Their marriage had settled into this predictable routine with Matthew either doing overtime or working on the house the last few months of their marriage. Many of their peers would probably consider this dull, but Raina liked the predictability. This meant her husband came home every night from his dangerous job.

Raina got dressed and went for her run. She waved to Frank and Maggie, who were walking the dog around Hook's Park. There was a lot on her agenda today, so she didn't stop to chat.

Before she hopped in the shower, she texted her grandma, asking if she wanted to tag along for a visit to the library. She got dressed, and while she ate her brunch, she checked her messages.

Po Po wanted to tag along to the library—which was a surprise after her explosion with the microfiche machine.

Her brother-in-law also called and left a voicemail. She tapped on the icon on her phone.

"This is Blue. I'm calling to check on how things are going. Do you need me to come up this weekend to resume construction? And did you talk to Matthew about our dad?"

Raina felt heat rise from her chest to her face. She had forgotten about her estranged father-in-law's request to join them for Thanksgiving. How could she broach the subject now to Matthew with all this going on at their house? At the rate things were going, they might not even finish the construction on time to host the dinner.

But she couldn't tell Blue no without asking her husband. Matthew hadn't seen his dad in over twenty-five years. Maybe he would want to see his dad after all this time. And maybe pigs grew wings. No, her husband would not welcome his estranged father to his first dinner party in his new home. And yet, Blue had worked on their house on his personal time, passing on the discounts for materials and arranging for subcontractors.

Raina took the chicken way out. Instead of calling Blue back, she texted him.

POLICE HAVEN'T SAID WE CAN RESUME WORK YET. I HAVEN'T TALK TO MATTHEW YET EITHER. SORRY.

Blue replied immediately.

OKAY. KEEP ME POSTED. I'LL GO VISIT DAD AT THE HOSPITAL THIS WEEKEND THEN.

Raina stared at the text message. Hospital? This explained the sudden desire to mend fences with his eldest son. She should stay out of this. Her fingers hit the send button before she was even aware of what it said.

IS HE OKAY? IS THIS WHY HE WANTS TO SEE MATTHEW?

She winced at the message. Great. Now she just got involved. There was too much on her plate already. What was she thinking?

And that was just it. She wasn't thinking. She was reacting with her heart. If it were her dad, she would want to see him, especially if he was sick. But Matthew didn't have the same relationship with either of his parents. He wouldn't like her interference.

Blue replied back.

I DON'T KNOW. I GUESS ALL THE DRINKING FINALLY
CAUGHT UP WITH HIM. HE'S IN A HOSPITAL IN LAS
VEGAS.

This explained how Wayne Louie was able to
attend their wedding. She replied back.

AND HE WILL BE WELL ENOUGH TO COME FOR
THANKSGIVING?

A second later, her phone buzzed with an incoming
message.

I THINK HE'D DIE TRYING.

RAINA FINALLY LEFT her apartment and drove over to
the senior condo complex. Once again, her grandma
was already waiting for her at the curb. Po Po had on
her "little old lady outfit"—elastic waist pants, blouse,
and cardigan with the pearl buttons. She even clutched
a normal-size black leather purse.

Po Po slid into the passenger seat, and Raina pulled
away from the curb.

"You have nothing to say about my outfit?" Po Po
asked.

"Nope. I figured you are probably trying to sway

the voters. You're going over to the dark side and pretending to be respectable," Raina said.

Po Po snorted. "All the candidates have to make a speech in front of the director and the Board this afternoon. There are times when you have to fit in." She sounded glum at the prospect.

"Just think of it this way. It's like a job interview. Once you pass probation, that's when your true colors come out."

Po Po brightened at the thought. "True enough. I can channel my inner Smelly Tally."

Raina averted her gaze to hide her smile. Only her grandma could turn a volunteer position into a dramatic stage production.

Po Po gave Raina a sideways glance. "Are you okay? You sound like there's something on your mind."

Raina thought about her conversation with Blue. While she would like to confide in her grandma, she knew what Po Po would say. If Wayne Louie were in a hospital, and if his illness turned out to be terminal, this might be Matthew's last chance to make amends with his father. And of course, the only way to find out if the illness was terminal would be to reach out. Raina wasn't ready to do the reaching.

"I need to let this marinate for a while. Talk to you about it later," Raina said. And hopefully, after they saw this case and the house construction was back on track.

"I'm always ready to listen," Po Po said.

The library was ten minutes outside of the downtown area next to a park with a Western-themed play-ground area. The building was U-shaped with a water fountain in the courtyard in the middle of the U. The left wing housed a café and a one-room bookstore run by the Friends of the Library, which was mostly staffed by volunteer senior citizens. A large meeting room and the restroom facilities filled the right wing. This meeting room often hosted movie nights, game nights, and arts and crafts for the local teen population.

They stepped through the automatic double doors into the library at the center of the building. The librarian and a volunteer were checking in books at the counter. The faint peals of childish laughter drifted over to greet them. It must be story time for the toddlers and children too young for school.

Raina made a right and headed toward the rear of the library, where the last two shelves were devoted to the yearbooks. Po Po tucked her head and followed, trying to avoid looking at the librarian.

"Miles probably went to high school in the late eighties or early nineties," Raina said, staring at the spines.

"I'll start in the eighties, and you can start at the opposite end. At least there is zero chance of this blowing up on us," Po Po said.

Raina gave her grandma a sideways glance. There was always a chance of something going wrong with her grandma around. She got down to the floor and pulled out the first yearbook. She might as well get comfortable because she would be here for a while.

Po Po opted for hunching over the shelves. For the next ten minutes, her grandma flipped through the pages of several yearbooks. She rubbed the small of her back and stretched. "It's time for a break. I'm going to join story time."

Po Po left, leaving Raina gaping after her back. So much for her wing woman.

Raina diligently flipped through the pages, glancing at the "L" names for each class. She hit pay dirt in the 1989 yearbook. She found Miles Lutz in the senior class lineup.

The boys wore a black tuxedo with bow tie, and the girls wore a white off-the-shoulder drape trimmed with faux fur that had seen better days. A dead rabbit scraped off the side of the road would probably look better than the grey fluff. She didn't understand the fashion in the 80s.

Miles had ginger brown hair, brown eyes, and a round friendly face. He had a mole underneath his right eye. This was the face of someone with a bright future ahead of him—someone who could be a productive member of their community. Instead, a few years after this photo, he was killed and hidden in an empty house. Poor thing. Why would someone kill this young man?

And to make matters worse, the killer escaped justice for the last thirty years. This was so unfair. If Detective Sokol was too lazy or incompetent to get justice for Miles, then Raina would have to take care of it.

Besides, until someone caught the killer, Miles's spirit would linger in her house. To some people, this may sound woo woo, but being Chinese, Raina had a healthy respect for the supernatural.

Raina flipped back to the beginning of the yearbook, searching for more photos of Miles. Student life from thirty years ago was no different than student life now. The clothes were stranger—big shoulder pads and pants that looked like they came from a genie. Almost every girl teased her hair until it rose like a crest on top of her head. Strange.

She paused, squinting at a group photo. A tall girl with ebony skin had an arm flung around the shoulders of Miles, who stood half a head shorter. Even at this age, the girl favored light colors—acid-washed jeans, a cropped T-shirt, and white sneakers. The only person Raina knew in town with this height and skin color was her former real estate agent.

Raina flipped back to the senior lineup, her finger sliding across the page under the names. Wackman. Wakefield. West. Iris West had gone to high school with Miles Lutz. What were the odds that this was the girl he was trying to help before his death?

Her eyes widened. Iris's parents must have been the previous owners of her house. She was the lynchpin that got Miles killed. How come the real estate agent didn't say anything about this?

14

AN UNEXPECTED NOONER

Footsteps approached Raina, and she glanced up to see her grandma standing in front of her.

"It looks like you found something, Sherlock," Po Po said. "Man, my timing is just perfect. Show me what you got."

Raina showed her the group photo in the yearbook and told her what she suspected. She tapped on the photo. "Here is the link between Iris West and Miles Lutz."

Po Po whistled. "Oh, I am going to love the look on her face when we call her out on it."

Raina frowned, going over her conversation with Iris at the Venus Café. "She was interested in the age of the remains. And she was upset when I told her they were probably about thirty years old." She told her grandma about Iris popping the lid off of her coffee cup.

"There you go! What more evidence do you need?" Po Po said.

"Whoa! There's a difference between withholding information and actually being the killer. Let's not be too hasty in jumping to conclusions."

"But you specifically asked her for information about the former homeowners, and she didn't tell you that her parents used to own the house."

"Actually she said that the former homeowners' information is not in the paperwork. Technically, I don't think she lied. She just didn't give us information that she already had."

Po Po waved aside Raina's objection. "That's just all semantics. She's still hiding something."

Raina pulled out her cell phone and noticed that she had a missed call. "Strange. Matthew just called me." She tapped on the voicemail icon and listened to the message.

When Raina hung up, Po Po asked, "What did he want?"

"He said he needs to talk to me right now. At home." Raina glanced at the log for the phone call. "He called just five minutes ago. We better get going. I can drop you off at the senior center."

Po Po wiggled her eyebrows at Raina. "Did he just call you for a nooner?"

Raina blushed. Her husband had sounded upset. She doubted he wanted what her grandma was implying. "You know who is obsessed with boobies? People who don't have them. Maybe this also applies to you,

Po Po. Are you going through a dry spell?" She put the yearbook back onto the shelf and got up from the floor.

"Honey, I have rechargeable batteries. There is no such thing as a dry spell for me," Po Po said.

Raina covered her ears with her fingers. "La-la-la-la. I don't want to hear this." There wasn't enough bleach in the world to get the image out of her head.

Po Po laughed. "Hey, you asked for that one."

"I was hoping it would embarrass you, so you'd shut up."

"You know I don't embarrass easily."

They got into the car, and Raina pulled out of the parking lot. At the curb outside of the senior center, she asked, "What time is your speech this afternoon? Is it at City Hall?"

Po Po rattled off the time.

"I should be done by then. I'll swing by to pick you up about twenty minutes beforehand. If I can't make it, I'll let you know," Raina said.

"Are you sure?" Po Po wiggled her eyebrows again. "I wouldn't want you to rush on my account."

Raina rolled her eyes. "See you later. Don't get yourself all hot and heavy. You might drain all the juice out of the rechargeable batteries."

Once Raina was back on the road, her flippant mood vanished. She rarely interacted with her husband in the middle of the day and never with an impromptu meeting like this. Whenever they had met for lunch, it was usually prearranged, with the caveat that Matthew might have to cancel at the last minute.

There were only two things her husband might want to discuss in private—additional bad news about their house or Detective Sokol's insurance policy. Butterflies settled into her stomach, and her hands tightened on the steering wheel. She wanted to turn the car around and drive in the opposite direction.

Raina parked in her designated slot next to Matthew's unmarked police vehicle. She strolled to her unit and hesitated outside her front door. She wasn't ready for this. She took a deep breath and unlocked the door.

Matthew was at the dining room table, eating a deli sandwich with a diet Pepsi and watching home improvement videos on his tablet. He glanced up and smiled, gesturing at the seat next to him. On the table in front of the seat was another deli sandwich and an iced mocha, the condensation pooling into a ring on the table.

Raina glanced at the gilded koi clock on top of the TV. One in the afternoon. She probably should have lunch, or she might get hangry. When she got hungry enough, they seemed to have more explosive arguments than usual. Matthew had learned it was best to feed her first before they had serious discussions. The butterflies in her stomach settled into a dead weight.

She locked the front door and joined her husband. In between bites, she brought him up to speed with the goings-on at the senior center.

"So Po Po is staging a coup and overturning the old

guard." Matthew shook his head in wonder. "What will she come up with next?"

Raina ignored his rhetorical question. And she kept silent about how his grandma and her husband backed away from investigating the murder. Now that they no longer had any potential of being in danger, he didn't need to know about their earlier involvement in questioning people at the senior center.

Matthew crumbled his sandwich wrapper and took another sip of his diet Pepsi. He flicked a glance at her half-eaten sandwich. "Not in the mood for meatball marinara?"

"I can't eat when I'm waiting for the shoe to drop. Just give it to me straight. What's the problem?" Raina asked.

Matthew sighed. "I don't want you to get hangry. I did try feeding you first."

Raina raised an eyebrow.

"Youri Sokol played a recording of a conversation between the two of you," Matthew said.

Raina hadn't expected Detective Sokol to approach Matthew with the recording. "What does he want?"

"For me to take a leave of absence. Youri seems to be under the impression that if I'm not around, he will become a superstar at the department."

Raina gave an unladylike snort. Did her husband mean delusion? "Fat chance of that. Without you around, Officer Hopper will outshine him in her sleep."

Matthew considered Raina's comment. "I never

thought of that. It would be a good opportunity for Joanna. Maybe management will realize they made a mistake with Youri."

Raina narrowed her eyes at Matthew. "I don't like the gleam in your eyes. I didn't say anything incriminating in the recording, did I?"

"Youri can file a grievance based on what you've said. They'll have to do an investigation, and I might have to take administrative leave for a few days until they straighten this out. I hope it's paid administrative leave."

Raina's hand flew to her chest as if to catch her racing heart. This explained why Detective Sokol used words like "harassment" and "bullying" in their conversation. He had planned something like this all along. She was such an idiot to fall for his trap. "I'm sorry."

"Done is done. And you know the worst part?"

Raina shook her head. If she spoke now, she might start crying.

"If the guys find out about this, they will not let me hear the end of it. It's one thing if I got my hand slap, but to get my hand slapped because of my wife..." Matthew gave her a crooked smile, his gold-flecked brown eyes twinkling with mirth. "Though I'm not sure why anyone would be surprised. I know you're trying to be June Cleaver, but we all know it's an act. Besides, you know that's not why I married you, right?"

Raina blinked at the burning in her eyes. The fluttering in her stomach disappeared, to be replaced by the fluttering in her heart. His words were a relief. She had been trying to be the perfect Chinese wife, a role her grandma had excelled at. It wasn't until after her grandfather's death that Po Po stopped pretending to be proper in public. In private, everyone in the family knew she was wackadoo.

"I want you to be proud of being married to me. I don't want to become a liability, but I seem to have failed." Raina paused and swallowed. Her voice cracked when she spoke. "I didn't see this coming. I didn't even suspect at all."

Matthew reached across the table and held her hands. "It's not the end of the world. Besides, overtime is not as lucrative as contract work. Maybe a leave of absence for a few weeks is not a bad idea."

"Then Detective Sokol wins," Raina said. She didn't understand where her husband was going with this.

"I don't care about Youri and his need to pee on the fire hydrant. I care about us, and what's good for our family. Right now, we need money for the house. We could probably resume construction again next week, but this delay will burn a hole in our budget. And who knows if the subcontractors can fit us in their schedule again? Like I said, contract work pays more than overtime."

Raina's hands tightened in his. "And it's also more dangerous. You're putting your life on the line in exchange for money."

Matthew gave her a deadpan stare. "How's that different than what I do every day?"

"It's different. I want you home with me at night, Matthew. When you're out of town, I worry constantly."

"This time, it'll be different. You have something to distract you. Just turn everything over to the police before the killer realizes you're on the trail. You can trust Joanna."

"I have no desire to play a superhero. That's your job."

Matthew smiled, crinkling the corners of his eyes. "Do you remember my buddy in Las Vegas?"

Raina nodded.

"He called me about a gig a few weeks ago. I declined at the time because we were busy with the house, but he called me again on the day you found the body—"

"I did not find the body this time. It was Po Po," Raina cut in. If she didn't set the record straight, he might think she actually enjoyed meddling.

Matthew ignored her comment. "As I was saying, I have been thinking about his offer. And with Youri requesting—"

"It's not a request. He's blackmailing you."

Matthew paused, considering her words. "You sounded just like your grandma. Those would be her exact words coming out of your mouth." He shuddered. "If you're gonna turn out like her, please make sure I'm dead first."

Raina smacked him on the bicep. "Really?"

Matthew widened his eyes. "Yeah. Make sure I'm

dead."

Raina chuckled, more out of obligation than any real amusement. He was trying to lighten the mood between them, and she appreciated the attempt. "So you're taking the job. When are you leaving town?"

"I'll put in my request this afternoon. I can wrap everything up and drive down to Las Vegas this weekend."

"Do I have a say in this?"

"Of course, you do. That's why we're discussing it now."

Raina leaned back in her chair, pulling her hands away from his. This didn't sound like a discussion to her. He had already made up his mind. Logically, she knew he was right.

As a former Marine who did special projects during his time with the feds, he had a lot of contacts in government. Whenever he took one of these contract assignments, they had always ended up with a nice windfall.

Raina didn't fault his logic or decision because they did need money. If only he could swallow his pride and let her ask her grandma for the cash. But then again, if he were okay with sponging off Po Po, Raina would not have married him in the first place.

She rubbed her temples. She didn't even want to know the reason why he had to drive instead of fly to Las Vegas. "Please just be careful."

Matthew got up and pulled Raina into a hug. "Always. I have too much to lose."

15

THE SHOWDOWN

Raina didn't remember much about what happened in the next hour. She must have picked up her grandma, and they ended up at City Hall for the campaign speech. Raina was functioning mostly on autopilot. The entire time, only two thoughts kept echoing in the loop around her mind.

Matthew is leaving. And we will lose the house.

When Po Po finished her speech, she plunked down next to Raina. The two of them watched Janice Tally make her speech, though Raina had no idea what the retiree said. Her grandma mumbled underneath her breath, but Raina wasn't paying attention to this either.

She was a strong woman. She didn't need her husband to make her feel whole and complete. But Matthew was leaving. And they will lose the house.

Raina's lower lip wobbled, and to her horror, tears ran down her face. When did she start crying? And in the middle of a campaign speech for the senior center. She ducked her head and used the hem of her shirt to wipe at the tears. It didn't do much. Her nose also became a leaking spigot.

"Here you go, Rainy," Po Po whispered tenderly. She held out a packet of tissues.

Raina pulled out several tissues, mumbling thanks. She blew her nose and wiped her face again. This was embarrassing. She glanced up to see Janice glaring at her from across the room. Heat rose to Raina's face. Oh, great. She probably interrupted the speech with her sniffling.

A few minutes later, after her grandma shook hands with members of the Board, they left the building. As the door began to swing shut, someone called out, "Wait! Hold the door, please."

Raina grabbed the door again and peered around it. Rushing toward the entrance were Janice Tally and Bucky Brown. Okay, rushing might not be the right word choice. Janice pushed the walker with a determined look on her face, and Bucky hovered close to her friend's elbow.

Po Po's eyes widened. "Here comes trouble. Just close the door, Rainy. We should get out of here."

Raina agreed with her grandma, but she couldn't shut the door on these senior citizens. It would be disrespectful. But neither did she want to be here when they had their showdown with her grandma. This was her fault for making all that noise during the speeches. She should apologize.

Raina handed her grandma the car keys. "Just go to the car. I will catch up with you in a few minutes," Raina said, holding onto the door.

"I am not deserting you at a time like this. We're in this together. If you're going down, then I'm going with you," Po Po said.

Raina suppressed the urge to roll her eyes. Her grandma could be melodramatic sometimes. "We have places to go and people to see. I still got to check on the house and try to track down Iris West. I don't have time for a spitting contest between you and Janice. Now go."

Po Po harrumphed. "It's Janice's lucky day. If not for you, I would give her a piece of my mind." She spun on her heels and left.

By the time Janice got to the front door, she was huffing and ready to chew nails. She peered around Raina to the plaza in front of City Hall.

"Where is your grandma? I know she's behind this. I can't believe she would make all those noises when it was my turn to speak. You didn't see me doing that when it was her turn. She is so rude." Janice spat the words out. As Janice spoke, she got more agitated, inching closer to Raina's face.

Raina suppressed the urge to wrinkle her nose and backed away. She could smell the little old lady scent that her grandma had complained about earlier. The mothball and the rose paper scent wasn't an unpleasant smell, but her grandma was so dead set against it that Raina couldn't help but react negatively toward it.

"I am so sorry," Raina said. "I had an argument with my husband earlier, and it came out in the middle of your speech. It had nothing to do with my grandma. The fault is completely mine."

Janice narrowed her eyes at Raina. "I don't know what Bonnie did to deserve a good granddaughter like you. Honey, you don't have to cover for your grandma. She is such a cow—"

"Any news on the discovery at your house?" Bucky cut in.

Raina shook her head. She appreciated Bucky's attempt to change the subject. "Not a thing. The police are playing this one close to the chest."

"They haven't even identified the victim yet? Wow, I don't remember them being this inefficient when my husband was mayor," Bucky said.

"When was this?" Raina asked.

"In the nineties. They were the power couple back then," Janice said, beaming at her friend. "They made things happen for this town."

Bucky blushed. "It wasn't like that." She glanced at her watch. "We need to go, Janice. We've got to pick up those fliers before the printer closes, or we can't get them until Monday."

Janice glared at Raina once more. "Tell your grandma this ain't over." She headed out the door with her friend.

When Raina got to the car, Po Po was sitting in the passenger seat with all the windows rolled down, playing with her cell phone. She glanced up guiltily at

Raina as if she got caught doing something she wasn't supposed to do.

Raina got into the driver's seat, ignoring the look. She didn't want to get involved in whatever her grandma was up to at the senior center. She already had plenty on her plate.

She started the car and drove to her house. During the five-minute drive, her grandma looked at her expectantly. When they got to the house, Raina pulled into the driveway and parked but didn't get out.

Raina told her grandma what happened during lunchtime. She gave her grandma a crooked smile. "So, that's my nooner."

"You know what mistake you made? You should start stripping as soon as you step through the door. That would have kept him busy for the rest of lunch, and he would have delayed the discussion until later," Po Po said.

Raina smacked her forehead with her palm. "Po Po, focus. That's not the point of this conversation. Matthew is leaving town this weekend and taking a leave of absence because Detective Sokol is blackmailing him."

"You shouldn't negotiate with people like him."

"I agree, but this is not my career. If this is what Matthew decided, I have to support his decision."

"If this happens once, you know it will happen again."

Raina nodded. "I don't expect it to be otherwise. But what can I do about it? It is all my fault."

"You still have the option to hack into his phone and delete the recording," Po Po said.

"Believe me; I am tempted. But I can't stoop to Detective Sokol's level. I need to do something to force him to delete the message without compromising my principles."

"Here is where the rubber hits the road, Rainy. What kind of person do you want to be? The righteous hero who always does the right thing, or the anti-hero who sometimes bends the rules. In my opinion, the anti-hero is just plain more fun."

"I don't think I have it in me to bend the rules. I might do a bit of eavesdropping and snooping, but that's because I'm nosy. But to purposely do something like invading Detective Sokol's privacy is more than I'm willing to do."

"How is it any different than all the Internet sites tracking your every move? There's no such thing as privacy anymore."

"I understand this. And here's the part I'm ashamed to tell anyone. Secretly, I am okay with Matthew taking on this side gig. Like he said, it pays a lot better than overtime. He's good at what he's paid to do, so even though I worry, I know he'll be fine. And we need the money for the house."

"Rainy, you know you don't even have to ask, right? All you got to do is accept it, and I can give you some money for the house."

Raina reached and squeezed her grandma's hand. "I know this. If it were just me, I would take it in a heartbeat. I don't know what kind of person this makes me, but I'm okay with my family helping me out. But with Matthew, it's different. He wants us to do it on our own, and I won't go against that."

"It makes you someone who knows her worth to her family. As for Matthew, I respect him, but he is making things harder than it needs to be. I don't understand this Lone Ranger American mentality. Back in China, that's the whole point of having a large extended family. It's a safety net, and everyone helps each other to build more wealth for the next generation. I can't take the money to the grave."

Raina nodded. She had heard this comment all her life. But Matthew's family came to America to build the railroads several generations ago, and he certainly had the Lone Ranger down pat.

"What are we doing here?" Po Po said, glancing at the house.

"It's been a few days. I want to clean up after the police. Wipe off the finger dusting powder and stuff," Raina said.

"Are you sure we can do this? I would hate for us to clean up, and then the police have to start over on whatever forensic stuff they have to do."

Raina frowned. She hadn't thought of that. "We'll take a quick look around, and then I'll call Officer Hopper to see what the status is. Right now, I can't talk to Detective Sokol without biting his head off."

They got out of the car, and Raina unlocked the front door to her house. She wrinkled her nose at that empty house smell—stale air, sawdust, and a trace of mildew.

The two of them stood at the doorway as if waiting for someone to jump out and shout boo.

"We should probably do a cleansing ceremony once we can resume construction," Po Po said uneasily, her eyes roaming around the hallway. Her grandma was more superstitious than she usually let on, but who could blame her? She grew up in the land of ghosts and dragons. "We have to balance the feng shui in this house."

Raina nodded. Anything to get rid of the bad luck associated with this house from the previous owners and Miles's death. "Please take care of it. It gives me the heebie-jeebies knowing what I do now."

"And you still want to live here?"

"Undoubtedly. It's the perfect location and size for our needs. It's not the house that is inherently off; it's the energy. All we gotta do is get rid of it."

"Which you can probably do by first finding out who killed Miles so his spirit can rest," Po Po said.

"I'm trying. At least now we have another lead. We'll start digging into Iris West's background."

"I can't believe the woman is fifty years old. I thought she was in her late thirties. And I thought Asians have good genes."

"Can you ask around at the senior center to see if her parents are still around?"

Po Po nodded. "Now wouldn't it be strange if they were members of the senior center."

Raina's eyes widened. "Promise me you will not approach them on your own. Please wait for me."

"If they are part of the senior center, they're probably over seventy. I can take them on." Po Po flexed her bicep. "I'm fit enough to teach the senior aerobics class."

Raina did not doubt that her grandma was fit, but it was known that desperation gave people strength. And besides, Iris might snap her grandma like a twig to protect her parents.

"You're like the muscle man at the circus. It's not your strength I'm concerned with. I don't want to accidentally spook them into flight," she said.

"Oh, all right. Besides, I don't feel quite right without my Posse Club," Po Po said.

Raina straightened and lifted her chin. "I'm going in. She marched to the entryway of the living room. She peered into the inside. "What the…"

Po Po was one step behind her. "Did somebody set up dust bombing here?"

The entire living room was covered with a fine layer of white dust—the windows, the fireplace, the floors, and even the wallpaper. The only area not covered by the dust was the exposed studs where the remains were found.

Raina's heart sank. If the rest of the house looked like this, she would have to hire cleaners to get rid of the dust.

Po Po patted Raina's shoulder. "I'll check the

kitchen and the backyard. Why don't you go upstairs and have a look?"

Raina nodded numbly. She had no words for how to describe what she was feeling. And she was afraid that if she started speaking, she would curse at the top of her lungs.

As she marched upstairs, puffs of dust swirled around her shoes. Even though they were done with the remodel upstairs, Blue had insisted that all flooring went in last. They were so lucky to listen to her brother-in-law. If this were her new carpet, she would have Detective Sokol's head on a plate.

Every room she went into was covered with the fingerprinting dust. There were several sets of footsteps everywhere. The whole thing didn't make any sense. Why would they dust on every surface? With Detective Sokol directing the case, she couldn't tell if this was an act of petty revenge or just plain incompetence.

Raina went back to the master bedroom, frowning at the pattern of footsteps on the carpet. One set looked methodical like the person was walking in a grid to cover the entire room. But the second set of footprints was random, going from the closet to the bathroom and back. The footprints smeared the dust as if the person was rushing and searching for something.

As soon as the thought floated across her mind, she couldn't shake it. But it didn't make any sense. Who would search an empty house? Or maybe the killer had hidden something in the house thirty years ago and came back to retrieve it?

Faint footsteps drifted up from downstairs. A heavy *tap, tap* that didn't sound like her grandma's orthopedic sneakers. Raina strolled to the railing and called out, "Po Po? Is that you?"

The footsteps stopped. The silence stretched for a long heartbeat.

The hair on the back Raina's neck stiffened. Her hands curled on the railing. The person downstairs was not her grandma. If this were a friend, he or she would have answered her back.

"Po Po, do you see Matthew's police car outside? He said he'd meet us here. He should be here any minute now," Raina called out.

She held her breath and waited. Her heart raced.

The footsteps came toward the front door. *Tap. Tap.*

At the top of the stairs, Raina was a sitting duck. Short of jumping out of the windows, she had nowhere to go. She pulled the pepper spray out of her purse and slid the safety off. She might be a sitting duck, but she wasn't going down without a fight.

16

A NEW DEAL

"Hello?" the familiar male voice called out. "Anybody here?"

Raina rolled her eyes. The intruder was pretending to notice someone was in the house with him. He was just as bad of an actor as her grandma.

The screen door at the rear of the house creaked open. That was Po Po coming inside the house. If she took a few more steps into the kitchen, she would see the intruder, who was probably in the hallway or the living room.

Raina clattered down the stairs with one hand on the rail to keep from breaking her neck in a fall. She jumped down the last two steps to see Chase McKenna in the hallway, and her grandma in the kitchen. Po Po held a nunchuck in one hand.

Chase swiveled from Raina to her grandma. His eyes were wide, and his expression startled. They had boxed him into the hallway. He took a step back until his rear hit the wall behind him.

He held up both hands, palms out. "Whoa! I'm here to check on the house. The paperwork you signed authorizes my being here." His voice was slightly shaky like he was afraid.

Raina sheepishly put the pepper spray back into her purse. "Sorry, we weren't expecting you. I thought maybe you were an intruder."

"Or the person who stole the power tools Blue left in the shed. All your wood flooring is gone, Raina," Po Po called out from the kitchen.

Raina shifted her gaze from Chase to her grandma. Who would break into the shed and steal their stuff? And how much would it cost to replace everything? "Stolen?" Her voice sounded muffled like there was something stuffed in her ears.

Po Po nodded. "I'm sorry, hon. I called Officer Hopper. She should be here in a few minutes."

Chase shifted uneasily. "Maybe I should come back at another time."

Raina stiffened her spine to keep from collapsing onto the floor and wailing. Everything was falling apart, but she couldn't show it, especially not in front of the bank vice president, who had the final approval on her loan extension. "No, please finish inspecting whatever you need to inspect. Can I answer any questions for you?"

Chase wiped his forehead with the back of his

hand. "I just want to see the progress and to take some photos for our files. I hope that's okay."

"No problem," Raina said. Might as well take care of the elephant in the room. She jerked a thumb at the living room. "This is where we found the remains."

"I'll wait for the police on the front steps," Po Po said.

Raina led Chase into the living room. She pointed to the removed drywall panel leaning against one wall. "As I said before, if we do run out of time, we can reinstall the drywall panel. We wouldn't have an open floor plan, but I don't think it will change the appraised value of the house. We'll have to replace the flooring and the carpet, and the house is ready for us to move in."

Chase snapped several photos of the living room. "What are your plans for the kitchen? Are you planning to replace the avocado green appliances?"

Raina shrugged, pretending a nonchalance she didn't feel. "It depends on how much money we have left at the end. What else do you need before you can make a decision on the loan extension?"

"Do you know when you can resume construction?"

"We can ask Officer Hopper when she gets here. She might have more information."

As soon as the words were out of her mouth, Raina cringed inwardly. It probably wasn't a good idea for the banker to have direct contact with the police. She had no idea what they might say or the impact of their words on the banker.

"Do you know if the police have any leads on this case? This situation is so bizarre," Chase asked.

Raina gave the banker a sideways glance. Was this casual interest or something more? "The victim is Miles Lutz, Phil's younger brother. Did you know him?"

Chase froze and licked his lower lip. A bead of sweat popped up on his salt and pepper temple. "I don't remember. It's been over thirty years."

Raina stiffened. How did Chase find out about the age of the remains? The police hadn't given an official statement on the case. "What has been over thirty years? Did you know the victim in your youth?" she asked carefully.

"No, no. I don't know Miles Lutz. I meant to say that he has been missing for over thirty years."

"I'm confused. If you don't know Miles, how do you remember him?"

"I just remembered the disappearance. It was such a big deal locally. Phil ran articles on his missing brother every week for a year. Long after the police had given up on the search." Chase flushed. "I'm embarrassed to say that I complained to my wife about the articles because it was irritating after the second month. They probably fought, and Miles just disappeared to punish his brother."

Raina narrowed her eyes. "A fight? So you knew

Miles well enough for him to tell you about a fight? I thought you didn't know him."

Chase lifted his hands and made the timeout sign. "Whoa! You're heading in the wrong direction. I don't know the Lutz family. When I said they could have fought, I meant theoretically. Brothers fight all the time. I don't know if they did or not."

"How long have you been working at the bank?" Raina asked, switching gears.

"My entire career. I love what I do."

"So you were working at the bank when they foreclosed on this house?"

Chase gave Raina an incredulous stare. "I don't even remember what I had for dinner last night."

"How could this house stay on the bank's books for all these years?"

"This might seem strange to a millennial, but before the widespread use of computers, we had paper files. The bank tried selling this property several times during the early nineties, but the country was in recession, and it didn't sell. Eventually, the files got packed into a box and shipped to our off-site storage facility. We recently found the files because we had to clean out our storage unit. This house is one of those properties that slipped through the cracks."

Raina bristled inwardly at his condescending tone. She hated being called a millennial. The word implied she was a fragile potted flower who couldn't survive in the real world. For someone who claimed not to remember what he had for dinner the night before, the banker sure knew the details on the foreclosure of this house.

Chase glanced at the smartwatch on his wrist. "I better take off now. I don't want to wait another minute to start my weekend. Keep me posted."

Raina walked the banker out of the house. She watched as he trotted down the driveway and onto the sidewalk. She lowered herself to sit next to her grandma on the stoop.

"Why did he park his car so far away?" Po Po asked.

"I was wondering the same thing." Raina told her grandma about why she'd thought Chase was a burglar and what they talked about in the living room. "All this time, I thought his interest in the case had to do with my loan extension, but now, I'm not so sure."

"This case keeps getting stranger by the minute. If everything was on the up-and-up, wouldn't Chase answer you when you called out?" Po Po asked.

Chase disappeared from their view. He must have parked the car at least a block away.

"My thought exactly," Raina said. "I think he was trying to sneak into the house and have a look around. If we weren't here, we would probably never know about his visit."

"Why is he here? I understand he can show up to check on the place, but why the sneaking around?"

"Good question. It had occurred to me that Chase is the right age to potentially be the banker who foreclosed on Iris West's parents thirty years ago."

"You're right. Is Chase a suspect? I don't see why he would kill Miles."

Raina shrugged. "I have no idea either...yet."

"Who do you think stole the power tools and your flooring?"

"Someone who wants easy cash. You can probably get rid of the power tools at a pawn shop and do a listing online for the flooring material."

"But who knows the house is under construction? You can't tell from the sidewalk. Phil's newspaper doesn't come out until tomorrow. There are rumors, but it's mostly talk at the senior center. I can't imagine any of us old folks moving Blue's miter saw and stand."

"Did you tell Ahanu?" Raina asked.

"I might have mentioned it to him, but he would never steal from you. He's a good kid." There was a hint of betrayal in her grandma's voice as if she was still considering the implications of Raina's question.

"Not him. But I wonder if he might have mentioned it to Chase's son, Forrest."

Po Po's eyes widened. "The opioid addict. Yes, that is a possibility. It will be hard to accuse him of this without proof."

"Can you get someone to install cameras around the property? We can spread the rumor more building material has arrived. You can contact Ahanu and let him in on the setup. Maybe we can catch Forrest in the middle of stealing again."

Po Po beamed at Raina. "I would love to set it up. Operation Sapling."

Raina chuckled. "Then we have a plan. Operation Sapling."

OFFICER JOANNA HOPPER showed up a few minutes later. She was dressed in her uniform, and her blonde hair was in a French braid. Her blue eyes and cherubic face were unreadable. Raina had never seen this side of the officer's game face before.

It took about twenty minutes to make a circuit of the house and the shed and discuss the missing items. After Po Po gave her statement, she offered to make tea in the kitchen.

Officer Hopper gave Raina a card. "Here is your case number. You can get an official police report in about three days. We'll call you if we have any information on the case."

"Can you catch the culprit who did this?" Raina asked.

"I'll talk to the neighbors and ask if they saw anything. Unless someone can offer information to identify the thief, we probably won't be able to find them. Sorry," Officer Hopper said. She looked apologetic like she was embarrassed by how little she could do to help them.

Raina debated for a half a second on letting the officer in on Operation Sapling but thought better of it. Until they had proof, she didn't want to spook Forrest

McKenna from returning to the house. It was better to catch him red-handed.

The two of them wandered back into the living room to look at the exposed studs.

"When can I clean all this up? We need to resume construction. Detective Sokol is not giving me any information, and it's been days. I don't want to file a complaint, but this is unacceptable," Raina said.

Officer Hopper frowned. "The forensics team was done a day ago. We had the county expedite this because Matthew is one of our own. Didn't Youri give you the message?"

Raina blinked. They could have resumed construction yesterday? She squashed down the surge of irritation. This wasn't Officer Hopper's fault. "Was all the fingerprinting dust necessary? It is in every room upstairs as well. Did you find anything?"

"I don't know. Youri is holding everything close to his chest."

"How much do you trust Detective Sokol?"

"I trust him with my life. He is my partner."

"Then he's one of the good guys." Raina hoped her doubt didn't creep into her voice.

"There are many shades of good," Officer Hopper said slowly.

Raina took a moment to digest the words. "I think I need your advice."

Officer Hopper raised an eyebrow. "Officially or offline?"

"Unofficially. As Matthew's friend."

"Let me guess. You want to keep this confidential as well."

Raina nodded. "I messed up this time." She told Officer Hopper what happened during the recording incident.

Officer Hopper blinked as if stunned. "Youri is blackmailing Matthew? The world is upside down."

"I know. If this weren't my husband's job at stake, I'd grab popcorn to watch the train wreck."

"Youri seems to have a lot of confidence that you can solve this cold case for him."

"What do you think I should do?"

"I don't think I am the right person to give you advice on how to handle this. You should probably talk to your husband."

Silence fell between them. The electric tea kettle whistled in the kitchen. Raina probably had another minute or two with Officer Hopper before her grandma returned to the living room.

"I'm more than willing to help investigate the case, but I am done helping Detective Sokol. He is never getting credit for my help again."

Officer Hopper raised an eyebrow. "Have you helped him before?"

Raina nodded. "We have teamed up previously." She gave Officer Hopper a sheepish smile. "It's my grandma's detective stories. It puts ideas into my head, and I'm nosy. The folks in town like to talk to me, so I know things."

Officer Hopper stared at Raina for a long moment

and sighed. "I probably shouldn't ask you this. I know I shouldn't ask you this." She paused. "Who is on your suspect list for this case?"

Raina hesitated. She wasn't trying to be coy, but neither did she want to show her hand yet. "How about we partner up on this, Joanna?" It was the first time she had used Officer Hopper's first name, and it was her first step at thinking about the policewoman as a friend and ally.

Joanna Hopper raised an eyebrow. "It took you this long to get over that I told Matthew about your involvement in the Merritt case?"

"Betrayal is a betrayal, even if I have to sit across from you at the dinner table once in a while."

"Yeah, but you trust me with your husband's life."

Raina shrugged. "So what do you think? Want to solve this together and knock Sokol down a peg or two?"

"What makes you think I'm interested? And since when do the police partner up with civilians? Even nosy ones."

Did Raina miscalculate here? "I thought maybe you would want to get back at Detective Sokol for his undeserved promotion. But if I'm wrong, we never had this conversation. I'll have to figure something out on my own."

Joanna held up her hand. "I didn't say I wasn't interested. I could always use an ally, especially one as resourceful as you."

They shook on the deal.

17

MOVER AND SHAKER

Raina spent the next few minutes giving Joanna Hopper the low down on the case. She told the officer about Chase McKenna's attempt to sneak into the house and his suspicious questions. She didn't mention anything about Forrest as the potential thief because she didn't want to compromise Operation Sapling. After all, there was no arguing with being caught red-handed.

"I also have the feeling that he might be the banker who foreclosed on the previous owners. I need to talk to one more person to get confirmation on this," Raina said, thinking about Iris West.

"Who do you need to talk to?" Joanna asked.

For some unknown reason, Raina was reluctant to pass on the real estate agent's name to the police. She had no proof of Iris's involvement in the case and didn't feel comfortable pointing the finger at her.

"I'm sorry, but I need to protect my source. I will let you know as soon as I know something," Raina said.

"I thought we were partners?"

Raina gave Joanna a pointed look. "And partners should respect each other's boundaries."

Joanna's gaze flicked back to her notebook. "So the banker is the only person on your suspect list? What about the victim's brother, Phil?"

"He isn't completely off my list, but he has no motive for killing his brother. The newspaper is a money sink. They've used family money to prop it up for years. There is no reason for Phil to kill his brother over a financial loss."

"You mentioned family money. How was this divided up before Miles's death?"

Raina blinked. She had assumed the newspaper was the inheritance, but what if it came with family money tied to it? This changed the equation and gave Phil a motive. "I haven't thought of it from that angle."

Joanna smirked as if pleased with stumping Raina for a change. "When you're talking about money of this magnitude, it's probably held in a trust. I'll see if I can dig up any information about it and how the money is distributed among the heirs."

Officer Joanna Hopper left shortly after. Raina locked up the house but gave the key to Po Po. Her grandma had asked her tech guy to come over the next morning to set up the cameras. Operation Sapling was underway.

AFTER DROPPING HER GRANDMA OFF, Raina went home to grill steaks and roast asparagus for dinner. Since she didn't hear otherwise, she assumed her husband would be home on time. If he was taking a leave of absence, he wouldn't stay to work overtime.

Matthew came home just as Raina was pulling the steaks out of the George Foreman grill. He sniffed appreciatively. "Now if this isn't heaven, I don't know what is." He strolled into the galley kitchen and kissed her.

Once Raina got her breath back, she asked, "Dinner in five minutes?"

Matthew nodded. "Let me wash up first."

"Did your boss approve the leave of absence?"

"Yes, and everything is all set for Las Vegas." He went into the bedroom.

Raina was putting the food on plates when the thought hit her about the timing of Matthew's trip. She had no idea how long he would be gone—and sometimes he didn't know either with these one-off gigs. However, his dad was at a hospital in Las Vegas, and Blue was also planning to be in the city this weekend. Would this be a good time for the Louies to have their family reunion? Or would the emotional fallout distract her husband from his job?

By the time Matthew emerged from the bedroom, she still wasn't sure what to do about the situation. The timing was too perfect not to say anything, and she had promised her brother-in-law to talk to Matthew. Their relationship was strong enough that she wasn't worried they would get into an argument. She was more worried about his well-being. Her husband had been in denial for years, but he hadn't gotten over his father's abandonment.

They ate in and made small talk about their day. When Raina told Matthew about the break-in at the house, he got upset just as she did.

"There is too much bad energy in the house," he said.

"Po Po will take care of it for us," she said.

"I think it's more than balancing out the chi."

Raina left out the part about the fingerprinting dust covering every surface of the house. It would only make matters worse. She didn't want her husband to worry about the house while he was working on a potentially dangerous side gig and dealing with his estranged father.

There was no point in asking for details. These jobs for the federal government were hush-hush, and apparently, as the wife, she didn't need to know.

"How did Detective Sokol react when you told him that you're going on a leave of absence?" Raina asked. If that jerk gloated, she was going to get back at him one way or another.

"He seemed surprised. I don't think he thought I would capitulate without a fight." Matthew chuckled, reaching for his beer can. "It was almost worth it."

"How much time are you taking off?"

"Three months. I figured after this job is done, I'll have time to work on the house with Blue. At this point, it's all hands on deck to finish even with the loan extension." His hand tightened around his beer can. "I think we need to ask your grandma for a loan, Rainy. The stolen flooring material is the straw on the camel's back. Even with the money from this job, I don't think we can do it without help."

Raina's eyes widened. "Are you sure?"

Matthew's expression was grim. "Yes, but let her know we'll pay her back with interest."

"Of course. Matthew, thank you. You've just made my grandma really happy."

Matthew frowned. "How's that?"

"Family is important to my grandma. And she has a very generous heart, so for her to watch us struggle when she could help, it breaks her heart. She doesn't show it, but it probably hurt her feelings that we weren't willing to take her money."

"I never thought of it like that before. I'm used to doing things on my own. I forgot that it's different for you and your family."

Raina reached across the table and squeezed his hand. "It's your family now too. You're one of us."

Matthew flushed and gave her a crooked smile. "I guess I am."

They resumed eating. Raina sliced and diced at the steak on her plate. She shouldn't bring up her father-in-law. Matthew seemed happy to realize that he was now part of the clan; she didn't want to break his small bubble.

But if something were to happen to Wayne before she spoke to Matthew, she couldn't live with herself. Family and closure were important.

"Are you dieting?" Matthew asked, pointing at the steak on her plate with his fork. "I think you look beautiful when you're enjoying your food."

Raina tried to laugh, but it came out as a snort instead. She flushed. "Now, that is embarrassing."

"What's on your mind, sweetie?"

Raina studied him for a long moment. She loved his gold-flecked brown eyes. His stoic personality kept a lot of his feelings under wraps, but Raina knew he could hurt just as deeply as anyone else.

She took a deep breath. Might as well get this over with. "Do you remember that elderly gentleman I saw at our wedding in Las Vegas?"

Matthew shook his head. "He already left the chapel when I turned around. Why are you thinking about him now?"

"Because I recognized him. He was your father."

Matthew's fork fell out of his hand. It clattered onto the plate. "My dad?" His voice was shaky.

Raina nodded. This was the most awkward conversation she had in a long time. "I think your grandma might have invited him to our wedding." She swallowed. "Blue will be in Las Vegas this weekend...to visit your dad at the hospital."

The ticking koi clock filled the silence between them.

Raina gave him a sideways glance. His expression was as cold as a slab of granite. She swallowed again. This was the part where the messenger got killed. "Maybe you can drive down a day early to check on Wayne."

By this time, the tension in the room was so thick, Raina felt like there was a rock on her chest. She stabbed at the steak on her plate and shoved it in her mouth, chewing vigorously. The marbling on the steak started out rich and buttery but now tasted like a lump of wet toilet paper. When could she be done with this meal?

She had delivered the message. Now the rest was up to her husband. It was his decision whether or not he would visit his dad. Her job was to support his decision, whichever one he made.

Matthew picked up his fork with a shaking hand and resumed eating. After two bites, he set his fork down. "Rainy, thanks for telling me." His voice was gravelly and thick like he had a stuffy nose.

She reached across the table and held his hand. "Do you want me to come with you?"

He shook his head. "It's okay. Just take care of things here."

Raina swallowed the lump in her throat. She wasn't sorry that she told her husband about his estranged father, but she was sorry that she wouldn't be able to help him through it. He had to do it on his own, and there wasn't much she could do about it.

But after he left, she was spreading the pressure around. Someone was responsible for Miles's death, and she wanted this person to worry just like she did for the last few days. They said misery loved company, and she was more than willing to share her misery.

THE NEXT MORNING, Matthew drove Raina, Maggie, and Frank to South Sacramento for dim sum. Po Po declined the outing, claiming she was busy with the Science Ninjas. While this might be the truth since she was directing Operation Sapling, Raina also knew her grandma didn't think the dim sum restaurants in Sacramento were up to par with the ones in San Francisco.

During the forty-minute drive, they made small talk. The two retirees did most of the talking, getting the two young people up to speed on the goings-on at the senior center.

"The Board is doing a full investigation into how the director is handling the money," Maggie said.

Raina hadn't heard about this part. "Will they get rid of her?"

Maggie and Frank glanced at each other, communicating something. Then Frank shrugged.

The corners of Maggie's lips curled, and she said, "Maybe you should ask your grandma this question."

Frank chuckled, enjoying a secret joke.

Raina frowned. She didn't like the sound of this.

After lunch, they took the retirees to Old Sacramento to walk along the river. It was pleasant and leisurely, and Raina got to hold her husband's hand the entire time.

After dropping the retirees off, Raina and Matthew went back to their apartment.

"I better start packing. I want to get on the road before it gets too late." Matthew glanced at her as if waiting for her to get upset. His original plan was to leave the following morning so they could spend more time together.

Raina turned on the laptop and grabbed a stack of bills next to it. "Sounds like a good idea."

Matthew didn't explain his decision to move up his departure time, and he didn't need to. Raina knew he was keeping his options open. During the long drive, he would mull this over. And if he did decide to visit his father at the hospital, he had a whole day to do it.

As they said their goodbyes, Matthew held her for a long time. They kissed until Raina became light-headed, and he left. She went back inside and glanced around her apartment with a critical eye. They needed to move into the house.

Her four-hundred-square-foot apartment was perfect...for just herself. When she signed the lease, she had thought of the place as a temporary situation. Somewhere to rest her head at night while she was in graduate school.

And now years later, with her degree in hand, she was still here and with her husband. Since Matthew moved in, she felt cramped and off-balance. They were stuffed to the gills with his things.

Raina knew Matthew always took care of his stuff, but she didn't realize how emotionally invested he was in his things until they moved in together. Maybe this personality quirk came from being abandoned as a child, and so his possessions were things he could control.

He was not quite a hoarder yet, but this could potentially be an issue in the future. When he moved in, Raina took it as an opportunity to clean out her apartment. Matthew, on the other hand, rented a storage unit.

She took a deep breath, mentally rolling up her sleeves. It was time to rock and roll. First, she called her grandma.

"Do you need me to come over to the house?" Raina asked.

"Nope. Everything is going great," Po Po said. "You can come by tomorrow to check the cameras. I've already talked to Ahanu. He is tutoring Forrest this afternoon, so he will mention the house got some new deliveries. By tomorrow night at the latest, we might have us a show."

Raina hung up, hoping her grandma knew what she was doing. The last thing they needed was for Forrest to trash the house because there wasn't anything left to steal.

Next, she called Iris West. It went immediately to voicemail. Raina wasn't surprised. The real estate agent wouldn't be happy to hear from her.

"Iris, this is Raina Louie. I need to talk to you in person. How come you didn't tell me that your parents were the previous owners of my house? The police might find this information interesting because the victim probably died back when your parents still owned the place."

Iris would call her back. She wouldn't want the police harassing her elderly parents. The real estate agent wasn't even a suspect, but she was connected to the case through her former relationship with Miles. She might have information that could point to the killer.

Raina grabbed the notebook from her purse and flipped through it to look at her murder notes. Something was bothering her, and she didn't quite know what it was. What did she miss?

She had already explained her suspicions to Joanna about Chase McKenna's ulterior interest in the case. But what about Phil's comment about the shady politician? She underlined the word "politician" in her notes.

Raina's cell phone dinged with an incoming text message from Iris West.

Venus Cafe in fifteen minutes.

18

TURNING THE TABLES

When Raina got to the Venus Café, it was in the middle of the dinner rush. She scanned the restaurant but didn't see Iris and stepped back onto the porch. Good. Maybe Raina could head her off by the front door. It might be wiser to have their chat outside on the porch of the restaurant or go someplace more discreet.

Raina wasn't someone who liked to play cloak and dagger games—that was her grandma's forte—but neither did she want her business advertised to the residents eating at the café. Some of the residents probably knew that Iris's parents were the former owners of Raina's house. Once they were seen talking, and if Iris had information, then the two of them could be potential targets for the hidden killer.

She glanced around. The front porch was lit up, so everyone inside could see them. Maybe they should have their chat on the path that led to the back of the restaurant. She got off the porch and checked out the path. Yep, this was perfect.

Iris showed up a minute later and climbed the steps to the porch.

Raina leaned toward the railing and called out, "Iris. I'm right here."

Iris jumped. "Raina? Where are you?" She stepped closer to the railing and glanced around in the dark.

"Down here."

Iris glanced down and jumped back. Her hands flew to her chest. "What are you doing in the dark?"

"Come around the side. I don't want people from the café to see us talking."

Iris's eyes glanced around uneasily. "This is silly. Who's going to care that we're talking?" She folded her arms across her chest, but instead of looking defensive, she looked like she was hugging herself.

"I need to talk to you. I don't want people to see us." Raina held up both hands, palms up. "Scouts honor, I'm not doing anything fishy with you in the dark."

Iris rolled her eyes and gave an exaggerated sigh, but she stepped off the front porch and walked around the side of the building until she was standing next to Raina.

"What's going on here? Your voicemail was quite sinister. It sounded like you were going to accuse my parents of killing some poor man and stuffing him into the wall of their house." Iris's voice was shaking, so the words didn't come out as forceful as she probably intended.

"I think you know the identity of the victim," Raina said.

"Why...why would I know him?"

"When did I say the remains belonged to a man?"

Silence.

Raina licked her lower lip. Time for the shock factor. If this didn't get Iris talking, nothing would. "You knew the victim. His name was Miles Lutz. Your former high school boyfriend."

Iris gasped. "He has been dead all this time after all."

"What did you think happened to him?"

Iris shook her head. "There was no trace of him. We searched for months. I figured he just left for one of the big cities. Disappeared."

"If he moved to another city, there would be a paper trail."

"Not in those days. It was easy to disappear. No Internet. No social media. You couldn't find people unless they wanted to be found. I thought maybe he just got fed up with his brother and left."

"Without telling you?" Raina asked, doubt lacing her words.

Silence.

"Miles said he would help me, but he had always been flaky. That was why we broke up in the first place. When I didn't hear from him, I thought he had moved on with another story," Iris said.

"And you never suspected foul play?" Raina asked.

"The thought had crossed my mind over the years,

but what else could I do? I'm not a family member. Not even a girlfriend. I had no evidence. I don't even have a potential suspect."

Raina's heart raced. No. No. No. This wasn't what she wanted to hear. "Why don't you tell me what happened. Start at the beginning. Why did the bank foreclose on your parents' house?"

"You are not entitled to my private business just because you're a previous client," Iris said, pulling herself to her full height and towering over Raina. "I don't know how Miles died or how he ended up in the wall of my parents' former house. But here's the keyword —it was a former house. The bank foreclosed on them, and there was nothing I could do to help them save it."

Raina stiffened but didn't back down. "Here's your chance to do something about it. Tell me what happened so I can help the police figure this out."

"You're kidding me. Why would the police be working with you?" Doubt laced Iris's words.

Raina hesitated. She didn't want to mention Matthew's name because her husband couldn't work on this case. Neither did Raina wanted to get Joanna Hopper in trouble. But there was one person she would gladly chuck under the bus. "I'm helping Detective Sokol."

"That man needs all the help he can get."

"Then you can see why I'm helping him. If I don't, I might never resume the construction on my house," Raina said, crossing her fingers in her pocket.

"It was so long ago. I don't see how it can hurt anyone now. My parents bought the house in the eighties during the real estate boom. They over-stretched themselves and couldn't make the balloon payment when the economy turned in nineteen eighty-nine. My dad lost his job, and we were surviving on my mom's part-time income. And when the oil prices soared, we just went under."

Raina frowned. The story sounded similar to the housing bust about ten years ago. But what did this have to do with Miles investigating a politician? "So how did Miles get involved in your parents' financial problems?"

Iris shrugged. "It was all my fault. I didn't under-stand the original paperwork for the sale of the house. It looked fishy to me, but I didn't understand it. So I asked Miles to help me look into it. He was smart at connecting the dots even in high school. By that time, he had his journalist degree, and he was working for his brother and also selling articles to other papers and magazines. I thought maybe he could find something to save my parents' house."

"And did he find it?"

"He probably did. That's probably why he's dead."

Raina ignored the sarcasm. She would circle back around to this later because Iris was getting agitated. "What was the relationship between Miles and his brother like?"

"I don't know if you would call it good. Miles felt

that Phil treated him like a child because he was the younger brother."

"Everyone knows the Lutzes supplemented the newspaper's operation with their own money. Do you know how this money was divided between the brothers?"

"Are you implying that Phil might have killed his younger brother for his share of the money?" Iris asked.

Raina shrugged. "The question had to be asked. Love, money, and revenge are usually the most common motives for murder. So do you think Phil might have done it?"

"I don't know. I met the man, but I don't know him."

"But you knew his younger brother. How did he talk about Phil? Was he respectful? Was he angry? I heard a rumor that the two of them might have argued just before Miles died." Raina had initially dismissed Chase's comment about the two brothers arguing, but there might be some truth to it.

"I don't think so. Phil was a new father at the time, and he was distracted. He basically left Miles alone to do whatever he wanted. As for the money, while they never flaunted it, money always seemed like an afterthought for the two of them. So I don't think money was an issue."

"But what happened to Miles's share of the wealth?"

Iris frowned. "Phil donated the money to build the

library. The previous one was in the basement of City Hall. It was only one room with a few metal shelves. The money paid for the land and building. And the leftover was put into a trust to supplement the funding for the library."

Raina had wondered how their little town was able to afford a modern library. It must have cost a couple million to build it. This confirmed her impression that Phil didn't kill his brother over money. "Was your parents' foreclosure the only one that Miles looked into?"

Iris shook her head. "No. There were hundreds of families in a similar situation."

"And they all took out a loan from the Gold Springs Community Bank?"

"I think so. Miles mentioned there was a connection, but I don't know what it is."

"He didn't give you a clue?"

"No. Miles said a powerful man was a silent investor at a bank. And these shady mortgage deals were a decent investment because the bank ended up with the house, the down payment, and the monthly payments at a time when the economy was turning."

"Could this powerful man be a politician?"

"Could be."

"Who was the most powerful politician in town? The mover and shaker?"

"The mayor?" Iris said. "I don't remember his name. Something Brown. He had connections with the governor's office. Or maybe he wanted to move into the governor's office. I don't remember."

Raina frowned. Wasn't Bucky Brown's husband the mayor in the nineties? According to Janice Tally, Bucky's husband was the Savior of the town. And she also asked questions about the case at City Hall earlier.

"How did Miles die?" Iris asked, breaking into Raina's thoughts.

"Head trauma with a blunt object," Raina said. "We found the murder weapon when we were cleaning up the backyard earlier today. Apparently after hiding the body, the killer was confident enough to just the toss the murder weapon out. I put it in the refrigerator."

She wasn't sure why she added the lie at the end, but it felt right. Like she was dangling bait to see who would snap at it. Even if Iris had nothing to do with Miles's death, she knew a lot of people in town and could help spread the rumor. It was time to force the hidden killer to step into the light.

"Aren't you supposed to notify the police?" Iris asked.

Raina shook her head. "Nope. Nothing is holding up the construction of my house again. I'll give it to them later."

"For all his flaws, Miles was a good guy. He didn't deserve to die the way he did, sealed up in a house, and forgotten all these years," Iris said, her voice thick with emotion.

"No, he didn't," Raina said. She felt a surge of anger

at the injustice of the situation. "The killer can't stay hidden forever."

"But how is that going to help Miles? It won't bring him back."

"But it will rest his soul."

The hair on the back of Raina's neck stiffened. Someone was watching them. She turned and looked up onto the porch of the Venus Cafe. Chase McKenna was sitting on the bench, smoking a cigarette. He was looking right in her direction, but maybe he couldn't see them in the dark. But he might have heard them.

Iris followed Raina's gaze and stiffened. Without another word, she ducked her head and trotted away in the opposite direction. It wasn't until she was moving that Raina realized this was the first time she had seen the real estate agent wearing a black outfit. The tall woman blended in with the night and disappeared from view.

Raina glanced back at Chase, who was now stepping into the Venus Café. She sighed. Might as well grab the bull with both hands. If he was the hidden killer, she might as well paint a large target on herself by approaching him. But he couldn't do anything to her in public. Besides, she had to pick up dinner for her grandma. With this logic, she strode into the café.

Raina stepped inside the Venus Café and scanned the area. She frowned. There was no sign of Chase. Either he was in the restroom, or he left through the back door. She trotted through the dining area and went to the little corridor that led to the restrooms and the back door. She stuck her head out through the door. A busboy was on the steps gobbling a sub sandwich.

"Hey, Mario, did a man go through here?" Raina asked.

With his mouth full, the busboy gestured to his left with the hand holding the sandwich.

"Middle age, white man. He's tall and bald. Is that the person?" Raina asked.

Mario nodded and swallowed. "Yep, he's wearing a dark-colored suit."

It looked like Chase had gone around the building and went back to the front. This also meant he had heard the conversation between Iris and Raina, and he was avoiding her. It was strange how the power had shifted between the two of them. Earlier, she was the one who was trying to avoid him. And now she would love more than anything else to question him more closely.

19

SMELLY TALLY

Raina went back inside and ordered take-out for her and Po Po. With Matthew out of town and folks starting to notice her interest in this cold case, it might not be a good idea to be alone in her apartment. Luckily, her grandma had a guest bedroom with the closet filled with clothes in Raina's size. Now, whether the clothing was her taste was a whole different question.

Raina texted to her grandma.

ON MY WAY TO YOUR HOME. SHOWING UP WITH DINNER FROM THE VENUS CAFÉ.

Her grandma immediately replied with several hearts.

When Raina knocked on Po Po's door half an hour later, her grandma flung the door open. She rubbed her hands together. "I'm so hungry. I could eat my foot."

Unlike Po Po's house in San Francisco, her grandma's condo was modern with tasteful furniture from Scandinavian Designs and bold decorations. Scattered throughout the unit were recent family photos. This home was a more authentic reflection of her grandma's soul than the antique furniture and fussy curtains in her Victorian.

Po Po bustled into the kitchen to grab plates and silverware. Though her grandma didn't cook, she didn't eat like a savage and insisted upon having a place setting if they were to dine at a table.

"Did you see the front page of the *Gold Springs Weekly*?" Po Po said.

"No, but I'm guessing that Miles's disappearance was on the front page," Raina said.

"And on the second page, and the third page."

"Was it just a report on finding his remains?"

"It's more of a celebration of Miles's life. His short life. Phil is offering twenty thousand dollars to anyone who has information leading to an arrest for his brother's killer."

Raina's jaw dropped. The reward money would turn up the heat in the search for the hidden killer. "If he's willing to offer twenty thousand dollars, I don't think Phil killed his brother."

"Unless he got more than twenty thousand dollars inheritance, and this is just a decoy to get the police off his scent."

"It's not like you to be so cynical."

"Fighting over money brings out this side of me. When my father died, all the ugliness of his multiple wives and children came out. I didn't have a mother to fight for my share, but the eldest wife, my Dai Ma, gave me enough money to get to Hong Kong. Luckily I had an aunt to take me in."

"And you met Ah Gong, so it worked out great in my book," Raina said. Ah Gong was the formal title for maternal grandfather in Chinese.

"Just so we're clear, I'm planning to have a good time with my money before I go. So don't count on getting an inheritance," Po Po said.

Raina laughed. She wouldn't want her grandma to scrimp and save to pass on the wealth like other Chinese families. "Loud and clear. Have a good time. Just don't expect me to come up with bail money."

They laughed.

Raina filled her grandma in on the conversation with Iris and the possible connection of Bucky Brown's husband to the case. "He might have been the shady politician."

Po Po nodded. "And that she was in on it. There was just something odd about that new girl. I mean, who can be friends with Smelly Tally?"

Raina grinned. Her grandma was probably jealous she couldn't wrangle Bucky Brown from supporting Janice. "We need to talk to Janice Talley after dinner."

Po Po's fork clattered to her plate. "You're kidding me."

"I'm sorry, Po Po, but you have to make nice with your arch-nemesis. She has the information that we need. I even bought an Apple cheesecake as a peace offering."

Po Po shook her head and folded her arms. "No way. I'm not talking to Smelly Tally. And you can't make me."

Raina switched gears. If she insisted, her grandma would only dig in her heels like a toddler.

"And I saw Chase McKenna at the cafe." She told her grandma about his disappearing act. "People are starting to notice that I am investigating the case. If we don't make progress soon, I'll become a walking target. Someone might want to shut me up, and I won't even see it coming."

This got Po Po's attention. "No one is going to hurt my girl on my watch." She picked up her fork, stabbing at the mushroom and cheese crepe on her plate. "Let's finish dinner and have dessert with Smelly Tally."

Raina suppressed a smile. "If you can't say something nice, don't say anything. Leave the talking to me."

"I will be biting my tongue the entire time. I have nothing nice to say to that woman."

They finished dinner, and Raina loaded the dirty dishes into the dishwasher and started the machine. She grabbed the cheesecake out of the refrigerator. The two of them left the condo unit, and they made their way to Janice's unit.

The fancy doorbell had a built-in digital camera and speakers. Raina pressed the doorbell, and the faint sound of a wind chime could be heard through the front door.

"She's not going to answer the door. She doesn't want to talk to us," Po Po muttered under her breath.

Raina ignored her grandma. The built-in speakers could probably pick up their conversation.

A green light came on in the doorbell. "It's late. What do you want?" Janice said, her voice crackling over the built-in speakers.

Raina held up the cheesecake. "My grandma bought you a peace offering. For what happened at City Hall earlier." She nudged her grandma with an elbow. "Say something," she whispered out the corner of her mouth.

"I'm not saying anything. I can't say anything nice right now," Po Po whispered back.

The front door cracked opened. The safety chain was in place, so they could only see a one-inch strip of Janice's wrinkled face. "Cheesecake doesn't agree with my digestion. I appreciate the thought, but I can't eat it."

"Can we come in for a minute? I want to talk about your friend Bucky," Raina said.

Janice frowned, or at least the one visible eyebrow furled. "I don't tell tales about my friends."

Raina leaned forward, glancing over her shoulders as if to make sure nobody was listening in on them. One thing she had learned from her grandma was that some senior citizens loved a bit of suspense to break up the monotony of their day.

She lowered her voice. "We're not here to gossip about your friend. We're here to save her from a police interrogation."

Janice's eyes flickered to Po Po and back to Raina. "If you can get Bonnie to behave, then I'll let you in."

Raina nodded. "My grandma has realized the errors of her wanton ways."

The door closed, and Raina turned to grin at her grandma, who scowled back at her. A chain rattled, and the front door opened again. Janice opened the door just wide enough for them to squeeze in one at a time. The three of them stood awkwardly at the small tile area, which served as a foyer.

Raina held out the cheesecake. "Are you sure you don't want to put this in the refrigerator? I made it this morning. Maybe your granddaughter might like a slice of apple cheesecake."

Janice hesitated for half a second and reached for the cheesecake. "I'll put this in the kitchen." She gestured halfheartedly at the living room loveseat and recliner. "Why don't you have a seat."

Janice turned and strolled into the galley kitchen.

Po Po marched over and sat down on the recliner.

Raina followed her grandma. "Po Po, you can't sit on the recliner. That's Janice's chair. Come sit next to me." She patted the cushion next to her on the loveseat.

"She didn't say I can't sit here," Po Po said, jutting out her lower lip. Her grandma was extra cranky because she was on enemy territory.

"The faster we get the information we need, the faster we can hightail it out of here. If you want to sit over there and start an argument with Janice, we'll be here even longer."

Po Po harrumphed but got up and joined Raina on the loveseat.

Janice returned to the living room and lowered herself onto the recliner.

It wasn't until she sat down that Raina realized Janice wasn't using her walker. Where was the medical equipment?

Po Po's eyes were scanning the living room, probably picking up on the same thought. Her lips were pressed into a thin line.

Raina sighed. Her grandma had always believed that Janice used the walker as a prop to appear more feeble than she actually was. And the knitting needles Janice kept in a little bag in front of the walker were used like cattle prods when it suited her. Please don't let her grandma say anything about the walker.

"Now, what's this business about Bucky and the police?" Janice asked.

Raina licked her lower lip. She would have to tell a white lie to get Janice to talk. Without a sense of urgency, her grandma's arch-nemesis might just kick them out. "We found the murder weapon while we were cleaning up the house, but we haven't turned it over to the police yet."

Po Po blinked but thankfully kept silent.

"I still don't see what this has to do with my friend. Why didn't you contact the police?" Janice asked.

"I don't want the police to shut down the construction again. We are already behind schedule, and if they had to shut it down again, I don't think we can finish on time," Raina said.

"What are you planning to do?" Janice asked.

"We took pictures of the weapon and stuck it in the refrigerator. We'll contact the police after we're done with construction."

Janice's eyes widened. "That's breaking the law. You're just as bad as your grandma."

Po Po bristled at the insult. Raina placed a hand on her grandma's knee to keep her from leaping to her feet.

"That's nothing compared to what your friend Bucky has done," Raina said.

"You can't go around making trouble for people. She hasn't done anything," Janice said.

"There is a rumor linking Bucky's husband with Miles's death," Raina said.

"What rumor?" Janice asked.

"Miles was investigating a story about a shady politician. And shortly after, he disappeared. It's too big of a coincidence that Miles died before he could reveal what he had found out."

"But that doesn't mean the politician is Bucky's husband. He formed a subcommittee looking into the Gold Springs Community Bank. If not for the former mayor, they might not have indicted the banker making those horrible mortgages with the balloon payments. Over five hundred families lost their homes, and a thousand more were on the brink of losing their homes. He was the town's Savior."

Raina wondered why Chase didn't mention the fraudulent banker. This wasn't something that happened every day. "What happened after the banker got hauled into prison?"

"It stopped more folks from getting their homes foreclosed on."

"I don't understand how this fraud thing works," Po Po said.

"Say the average house is three hundred thousand dollars," Raina asked. "If the homebuyer put down ten percent as a down payment, that's thirty thousand dollars. Multiply this by five hundred homes, and you have fifteen million dollars. When the bank foreclosed on the homes, someone pocketed the fifteen million, plus the equity, and the bank ended up with the house, which they sold off."

"But what happened to the money?" Po Po asked.

Janice shook her head. "It disappeared. The shady banker didn't have it. There were rumors of a silent partner for the bank, but there's no evidence such a person existed."

"So, the banker was the only one punished for the missing money?" Raina asked.

"The president at the time resigned, and everybody on the Board lost their job. But yeah, the banker was the only one who went to prison," Janice said.

Raina wondered if the banker was only a straw man, set up to take the fall. "What happened to the other homeowners on the brink of foreclosure?"

"The federal government helped them refinance," Janice said.

Raina's thoughts drifted to Iris's family. If only they had held on long enough, but then, maybe the bank fraud wouldn't have come to light. "I bet Bucky's husband must have won every election after this."

"Actually, he resigned after the investigation was over. Then they moved out of town," Janice said.

Raina gave Janice a sharp look. "Really?"

Janice scowled at Raina's tone. "What are you implying?"

"Did the former mayor endorse the bank in any way during his time in office? Was he associated with the bank?" Raina asked.

Janice's silence was confirmation enough.

Raina sat back on the loveseat. Did the former mayor point a finger at the bank to divert attention from himself? Maybe he was the silent partner who ran off with the money. And what was Bucky's level of involvement in all this?

20

OPERATION SAPLING

They left Janice's condo unit and strolled back to her grandma's home. Raina's mind spun as all the little facts added up. She would have to hurry, or they might miss their chance at catching several people red-handed.

Janice was probably on the phone with Bucky Brown to fill her in on the location of the murder weapon. Her grandma's arch-nemesis wasn't entirely convinced that her friend had anything to do with the murder.

Po Po trotted to keep up with Raina. "What's the rush? Is the house on fire?"

"I have to do a stakeout tonight, and I only have a few minutes to get ready for it."

Po Po rubbed her hands together with a big grin on her face. "Really? Where at? I'm in."

Raina would actually prefer her grandma to stay home. Undoubtedly, her grandma would guzzle Red

Bull the entire time they hid in her car. "I think you should sit this one out, Watson."

"No way. You're gonna need backup."

"I know. That's why I am planning to call Joanna Hopper."

Po Po's eyes widened. "When did you two become BFFs?"

"When we decided that we have a common enemy."

"Detective Sokol?"

"Yep. She'll crack the case and take all the credit. I will stand on the sidelines and laugh at Sokol's face when he realizes what just happened."

"You know this means he will turn over the recording to Matthew's boss."

Raina shrugged. "We don't negotiate with blackmailers. He will have to explain to the chief how he forced Matthew to take a leave of absence. Whatever the fallout, he's not coming off squeaky clean either."

"Now that's my girl. That's right. We don't negotiate with blackmailers."

They got to Po Po's unit, and she let them in.

Her grandma glanced down at her comfy white T-shirt and yoga pants. "How much time before we leave? I need to change into my stakeout clothes. I need to be able to blend in with the night."

Raina sighed. There was no point in arguing with her grandma. "How about fifteen minutes? I need to convince Joanna that something is going down at the house tonight."

She hoped something would go down tonight because she wanted to get back to her home construction. Unfortunately, she couldn't let this investigation go either. So the faster they wrapped this up, the faster she could get back to her normal life.

Raina called Joanna's cell phone number. It was picked up on the third ring. "Joanna, something is going down at my house tonight. Can you join me for a stakeout?" She explained that they spread rumors about new material deliveries and replacement tools. "The thief might try again tonight."

"You know I can't participate, right? This would be considered entrapment. As a police officer, I can't do this," Joanna said.

"But if you happened to be in the neighborhood when I call the police, can't you respond?"

"I'm not on duty tonight."

"What if you were in the neighborhood because you were visiting a friend? And you see something suspicious when you look out the window. Couldn't you respond then?"

"I don't have a friend that's across the street from your house."

Raina wanted to grind her teeth. Why didn't cops have more imagination? "I'm your friend. Maybe we are across the street, talking to each other, when the thief returns to my house again."

"What if we don't catch this thief until two in the morning? How do I explain this to my boss?"

"I don't know. Maybe we're coming home from a

bar. Friends do go out to drink together. Just use your imagination."

Silence.

"Are you in? Or are you out?" Raina asked.

"I'll see you in a few minutes."

Raina hung up and did a fist pump. Fantastic. Hopefully, they would catch Forrest McKenna in the act. If the killer did show up, then they would catch two birds with one stone. Someone was bound to come looking for the imaginary murder weapon in her refrigerator.

RAINA WAS SITTING in her car underneath the tree across from her house with the engine turned off. Her grandma was on the passenger seat, snoring away. It was midnight, and she was starting to think the stakeout was a bad idea.

She stared at the tablet on her lap and swiped at the screen to flip through the video feeds. Her grandma's tech guy did a great job, installing four cameras to cover all corners of the backyard. They had even installed a camera inside the shed, so they could capture the thief's face when he opened the shed. The backdoor's bulb provided just enough light to capture movement. The two cameras pointing at the driveway covered anyone coming up to the house. The front door light and the streetlight provided the illumination to identify the thief.

When Raina had explained the idea to Po Po, her grandma had suggested purchasing some decoy power tools for the shed. The boxes were filled with rocks to the approximate weight of the tools and padded with packing material so that they wouldn't rattle. The new equipment was sitting inside the house, some of them charging on the kitchen counter. The thief would probably grab what he could and dash off. He wouldn't take the time to open the box and inspect the tools.

Tap. Tap.

Raina jumped at the sound. She glanced at the window to see Joanna Hopper staring down at her. Raina rolled down the window. "Are you leaving now?"

"We've been here for four hours. I don't think anyone's going to show up," Joanna said.

"As a cop, I thought you had a lot of practice with stakeouts. You should know that sometimes the break doesn't come until hours later." Raina unlocked the door. "Come on in and join us. I have snacks and Red Bull. Or you can take a snooze like my grandma. I'll wake you if there's any action."

Joanna opened the door behind Raina and got into the car. "I'm going to regret this in the morning," she muttered under her breath.

Raina turned around until she faced the police officer. "Were you able to find out anything about the Lutz's trust fund? Was it tied to the newspaper?" Even though she already knew the answer, she didn't want to invalidate the work that Joanna might have done.

"Phil and Miles each had a trust fund of their own.

They were both financially well-off, so Phil probably didn't kill his brother for money," Joanna said, sounding disappointed.

Raina nodded. She already suspected this. She told Joanna about her conversation with Iris West—though she withheld Iris's name—and her conversation with Janice. "I think Bucky's husband was the silent partner at the bank, and Miles was onto him. His widow recently moved back to town because he died. What are the options when the murderer died before he was discovered?"

Joanna frowned. "I guess the district attorney could still seek a conviction to get justice for the family."

"And if I'm wrong about Bucky's husband, there's always Chase McKenna. When all these homes were being foreclosed, he was working for the bank. Isn't it odd that he didn't work on a single one of these loans?"

"What are you trying to say? Do you think they imprisoned the wrong banker?"

"Or maybe someone paid the banker to take the fall. We don't know unless Chase starts squealing."

"We have no leverage to make him talk."

Raina shrugged. "Maybe not...yet." If Forrest were the thief, then maybe they would have the leverage they needed. It was still too early to reveal the game plan. Cops liked evidence.

"I don't understand," Joanna said. "Why don't you focus on the construction? Why continue to pursue this investigation? Matthew would want you to drop this case."

"Yes, I know he would. But if the shoes were reversed, he wouldn't drop it either. Do you know why?"

"No, I don't."

"If someone were to threaten my job, he would go papa bear on them. He would protect me just like I am doing the same for him now. He sees the department as his family. He might let this slide because Detective Sokol is like an errant sibling. But I can't let this slide. I made the mess, so I will clean it up."

"I didn't think you had it in you to be this ruthless. Youri might get demoted for this. Don't you care what happens to his twin boys?" Joanna asked.

"They're old enough for his wife to get a job. It's not like he'll get fired. He'll go down a rank. They won't end up on the street," Raina said. She was tired of people using their children as an excuse for doing shady activities.

The sound of a car engine approached their location. Raina sat back into her seat and slumped behind the steering wheel. Joanna crouched low in her seat. Luckily, Po Po had her chair leaned back, so her head was invisible from outside the car.

A dark-colored pickup truck pulled up in front of Raina's house, parked, and turned off the engine. A tall man got out, wearing a black sweater with the hood pulled up and black jeans. He stood by the car, scanning the street.

When his eyes landed on the Honda Accord, Raina almost jerked back. It took all her willpower to stay put. The tinted windows in her car gave her more than sufficient coverage, but any sudden movement could give her away her location. Joanna stiffened and held her breath. When the man was satisfied, he turned and ran up the driveway. He disappeared around the side of the house.

A surge of adrenaline ran through Raina until it felt like even her toes were tingling. Their plan had worked! They were about to catch Forrest McKenna red-handed.

"We'll have to wait until he puts something into his truck, or it will be our word against his," Joanna said.

Raina gestured at the tablet. "Actually, we have video footage." She swiped through the various camera feeds, each of the cameras in the backyard showing Forrest approaching the locked shed.

Joanna gaped. "We don't have access to tech like this at our department. Our budget barely covers replacement computers." She gave the sleeping Po Po a sideways glance. "No wonder your grandma and her cronies at the senior center are always one step ahead of us with their mischief."

"This is an inner circle secret. If you want our help in the future, the stuff you see here stays in here," Raina said, drawing a circle in the air with her index finger. "Not even Matthew has seen this."

Joanna held up both hands, palms first. "Fair enough."

Raina cocked her head. What was that? She turned the tablet upside down, killing the light in the car. She held a finger to her lips and ducked back down into her seat. Joanna followed her lead and faded into the backseat.

A silver SUV glided slowly down the street and stopped when it pulled up next to the truck. The driver glanced at the house and rolled down the road until he disappeared from view.

"Now who was that? A nosy neighbor?" Joanna asked.

"Wha dat!" Po Po mumbled, jerking up from her sleep.

"Shhh! The thief is cutting the lock on the shed," Raina said.

Po Po's eyes widened, and all trace of sleep left her face. She glanced down at the seat pan as if looking for the button to move her seat upright.

"Don't move," Raina said, glancing out the windshield. "Someone is coming."

Everyone in the car froze. Raina tracked the approaching shadow on the sidewalk across the street. With the streetlight distorting the shadow, Raina couldn't tell if the approaching person was a man or a woman. But it must have been the same person who drove past in the SUV.

Raina frowned. Now that she thought about it, the car looked familiar. Where had she seen it before? At City Hall? No. At the bank? Yes, she had parked next to it. The shadow stepped into a pool of streetlight, illuminating Chase McKenna.

21

A SURPRISE VISITOR

Chase glanced at Raina's parked car across the street and turned his back on it. He walked up to the pickup, glanced at the bed, opened the driver's door, and got in.

"What do we do now, Sherlock?" Po Po whispered. Her eyes kept shifting to the tablet, probably itching to look at the video feeds.

"Now we wait," Raina whispered back. Her body ached from the hours of inactivity and the recent surge of adrenaline. She wanted nothing more than to throw open the door and march over to knock on the window of the truck.

"The suspense is killing me," Po Po whispered. She reached into her beach-size bag and pulled out her Taser and pepper spray.

Joanna shifted, and something metallic clinked. "Po Po, stay in the car when I confront the suspects."

Raina raised an eyebrow at the authority behind

the words. While she understood why Joanna wouldn't want a senior citizen in the middle of an arrest, that tone of voice would get her nowhere.

"I hope you have your gun with you. The two of them could easily take us down," Po Po said, ignoring the comment to stay in the car.

Movement from the side of the house caught Raina's eyes. "Here comes the thief. Shhh!"

Forrest stepped into the streetlight, carrying the box of a compound saw. While holding onto the box with one hand and balancing it on a raised knee, he struggled to open the tailgate.

Chase stepped out of the driver's seat. "What are you doing, son?"

Forrest jerked and lost his grip on the box. It crashed onto the ground. He jumped back, hopping on one foot. He cursed.

Joanna gasped in the back seat. "The thief is his son? The football star?"

"He's addicted to opioids," Po Po whispered.

"Shhh!" Raina shushed them. Was this the time to reveal their presence or wait to see how the drama played out?

Joanna scooted across the back seat and flung open the rear passenger door behind Raina. She barreled across the street with her gun out. "Police! On the ground, and hands where I can see them."

Raina gaped at the explosion of movement. Po Po pulled out her cell phone and dialed 911.

Forrest spun on his heels and disappeared into the night.

"No, son! Running will make it worse," Chase hollered after his son. His hands were raised, and he was on his knees on the sidewalk.

Raina recovered her senses and ran out of the car. What should she do? Should she go after Forrest? What if he had a weapon?

Joanna tossed her handcuffs at Raina, who caught them in midair. "Cuff him." She swiveled on her feet and ran after Forrest.

Raina focused on Chase, approaching him slowly. "I'm sorry, Chase, but you heard Officer Hopper."

Chase didn't resist when she snapped the cuffs on his hands behind his back. She carefully helped him sit crisscross applesauce on the sidewalk.

Po Po came out of the car with a blanket. She threw it around Chase's shoulders. "The cold from the ground will just go right through you."

The wrinkles settled in on Chase's face, and the dark eye bags had their own eye bags. "Thank you."

Raina kneeled next to him. "When did you suspect your son was the thief?"

Chase sighed, a deep bone-weary sigh. "I'm not talking without my lawyer."

"Hey, if you talk to me, you might not need a lawyer," Raina said.

This got Chase's attention. "You won't press charges against my son? He's a good boy. He just needs help. I didn't know about his addiction until a couple of weeks ago. He didn't have this problem before. It's the football injury from last year." By this time, Chase was almost babbling.

"I know all about his injury and addiction," Raina said.

"How?"

"People like telling me things, and I could put random pieces of information together. I also suspected your son when I found out that someone broke into the shed."

"I'm sorry. I'll replace what my son stole and approve your loan extension. Just give him another chance. He doesn't need to go to juvenile hall. What he needs is a rehab center."

Raina flicked a glance at Po Po. Her grandma shrugged as if to say it was Raina's call. Since there was no telling how many people Forrest might have stolen from, she didn't know how long he had been committing these crimes. "I won't press any charges for what he did at my house, but other people might come forward."

Chase closed his eyes as if in silent prayer. When he opened them, his exhaustion was even more visible by the dull sheen in his eyes. "That's good enough for me."

Raina didn't know how to bring up the subject of the home foreclosures gracefully, so she just went straight to it. "When Miles Lutz was investigating the home foreclosures thirty years ago, there was a rumor about a silent partner. Was this partner the mayor at the time?"

While Raina spoke, Chase grew more alert. He pressed his lips together as if to prevent himself from talking, and his eyes shifted. When his gaze returned to Raina, he blurted out, "Yes."

"How did you find this out?"

"I saw the bank president and the mayor at the old steel plant one weekend. I was hiking on the back roads. And when the rumor started of a silent partner, I was able to put two and two together."

"Were you involved in any of those deals?"

"No. I was too low on the totem pole."

"Then how did you find this information?"

Sweat popped up on Chase's upper lip. He appeared to be fighting an internal war on how much to tell her.

"You might as well tell me everything. It's bound to come out now that Phil Lutz is offering a twenty-thousand-dollars reward to find his brother's killer," Raina said.

"I didn't kill him."

"I believe you, but I think you have information," Raina said. From the corner of her eye, she could see her grandma moving closer to Chase. Was her grandma recording the conversation?

Chase's shoulders sagged. "I was his informant. We were supposed to meet the night he disappeared. I made copies of several loans for him. It was the paper trail he needed as evidence."

"What did you do when he didn't show up?"

"I went home. What else could I do?"

"How come you didn't come forward when he was reported missing?" Raina asked.

Chase stared at her like she sprouted another head. "I knew in my gut something bad had happened to Miles. I wasn't going to keep digging or make myself a target. Not against the town Savior. When they fired people and switched out the Board, I kept my head down and did my job."

Raina understood perfectly how he felt. Very few would be comfortable standing up to Goliath. And once Chase established himself in his career and got married, he had too much to lose.

"Will you come forward now?" Po Po asked, intruding on the conversation and breaking the bubble of confidence.

Chase huddled under the blanket. "Let me think about it. I have to take care of my son first, and I can't have the spotlight shining on us while we're dealing with his drug addiction."

"The former mayor is dead, but solving this cold case would finally give Phil closure over Miles's death," Raina said.

Chase closed his eyes and dipped his chin close to his chest, pretending like he was napping on the cold concrete sidewalk.

Approaching footsteps crunched on dried leaves. Raina glanced behind her and saw Joanna jogging toward them. Instead of stopping, she threw a glance at

Chase and kept going until she got to her unmarked car.

She opened the door and pulled out a hand radio.

"I think she's putting out an APB on Forrest," Po Po said. "She'll need backup to find the kid in the dark."

Chase's head jerked up, and he glanced at Joanna. "He's a good kid. Please don't let them shoot him," he mumbled to himself.

"It will be okay. Your son is not a juvenile delinquent. It's just a broadcast for help to track him down," Raina said.

Chase rocked back and forth. "There will be a search. They'll use excessive force. That's how it goes these days."

"There's a lot of good people in the world even though it seems like the bad apples get all the attention," Po Po said.

"Nobody in the department will kill your son," Raina said. "If you have any idea where he might be, it's better if he turns himself in. I am not pressing charges. He needs to cooperate with the police."

Joanna put the radio away and trotted over. "Chase, I need you to go to the station with me. I have some questions."

"I don't want to press any charges," Raina said. "Forrest is just a kid. Chase said he would get his son into rehab and reimburse us for our stolen items."

"What about my Miranda rights?" Chase asked. His tone was resigned rather than cocky.

"You're not a suspect. I'm assuming you came here

to stop your son from committing a crime," Joanna said.

"Fat good that did," Chase muttered.

"Are you coming to the station?" Joanne asked.

"Yeah, I'll come."

Raina and Joanna helped get Chase off the sidewalk. Once the banker was on his feet, he toddled over to Joanna's car. Joanna kept a hand on his elbow the entire time. He got into the backseat without resistance.

"I've got to take a few photos of the crime scene and the stolen goods on the sidewalk. I will be right back," Joanna said.

Chase ignored the comment and leaned back on the seat, closing his eyes.

Joanna closed the door. She opened her trunk and took out a small black bag. As they trotted back to the house, she turned to Raina. "Can you email me those video feeds?"

Raina nodded. "Do you need it right away, or can it wait until I get home? The wi-fi signal is better at my house."

"As soon as possible. It will make a stronger case," Joanna said.

"What will happen to Forrest? He's needs rehab, not prison time."

"That's for the judge to decide. Unfortunately, he has stolen expensive items. It's a grand theft."

Raina glanced at her grandma. "We're taking a look at the shed. You want to come?"

Po Po shook her head. "I'm going back to the car." She yawned. "I'll keep an eye on things out here in case the kid comes back."

They strolled up the driveway and into the backyard. The shed was wide open, most of its contents thrown on the ground. Luckily, the power tools were safe in the house, plugged into the outlets, and charging their batteries. Blue would be able to start working as soon as he walked through the front door of the house.

While Joanna took pictures, Raina filled her in on her conversation with Chase. The police officer took out her finger dusting kit from her black bag and worked on the shed.

"I don't think I'll be going to bed anytime soon, but I'll track down Bucky Brown later this afternoon," Joanna said.

"Do you want me to help you with anything?" Raina asked.

"You have more than done your part. Not only did we find the thief, but we also found out who probably killed Miles. I can take it from here."

Raina nodded. A wave of exhaustion swept over her. Poor Joanna. At least Raina could go to bed after this. "Will you keep me updated on the investigation?"

Joanna nodded. "I'll tell you what I can."

Joanna went back to the front of the house. A door slammed, and a car engine started.

Raina glanced at the mess in her backyard. The morning dew would ruin the baseboards and probably some of the other materials as well. She couldn't see well enough with the backdoor light to know what items to put away and what items to leave out until the next day.

She yawned, nearly cracking her face in half. There was a heavy-duty flashlight somewhere in the house. Might as well get the show on the road.

She opened the backdoor and flipped on the light. Her jaw dropped. Where was all the fingerprinting dust? Did a cleaning crew come in? A smile broke out on her face. Thank you, Po Po. Her grandma had just saved Raina hours of wiping everything down.

A quick rummage around the kitchen revealed no flashlight. Neither was it in the dining room or the living room. Maybe someone left it upstairs.

There was enough illumination coming from the kitchen, so she didn't bother flipping on the hallway light. At the top of the stairs, she flipped on the light. She went into each bedroom and finally located the flashlight underneath the bathroom cabinet. And like the rest of the house, the bathroom was dust-free.

Raina clicked on the flashlight. The battery was dead. All this searching for nothing. Cell phone light it was. If only she had an extra hand to hold it up for her while she dragged things back into the shed. She called her grandma, but after several rings, it went to voicemail. Oh, shoot. Her grandma fell asleep in the car. She glanced at the display on her phone. 2:30 A.M. Oh, what she wouldn't give to curl up in bed.

Her head jerked up from the phone. What was that

noise? She tiptoed to the landing area and glanced over the railing. Someone was in the house.

She put her phone on silent and texted Joanna.

"Forrest came back to the house."

The phone vibrated in Raina's hand. The officer replied immediately.

I NEED TO GET SOMEONE TO WATCH CHASE.

I'LL BE THERE IN FIFTEEN MINUTES. STALL THE KID.

22

POP GOES THE WEASEL

Raina didn't dare to flip off the lights. The teenager might notice a change in the lighting level in the house. The last thing she wanted was to spook the kid and have him take off again.

She could wait up here until Joanna arrived. But Raina had a feeling Forrest was doing a grab and dash. She had better go downstairs and talk to the teen. A long chat with a juvenile delinquent was on the bottom of her list of favorite things to do in the wee hours of Sunday morning.

She tiptoed downstairs, holding onto the defunct flashlight. The heavy weight felt comforting in her hands. At the foot of the stairs, she paused. What if the person in the kitchen wasn't Forrest? She dismissed the thought. What were the odds of someone else burglarizing the house?

As Raina approached the kitchen, a moving

shadow spilled out onto the floor and disappeared. She blinked. The shadow didn't look like a lanky teenager. She stepped into the kitchen, and her jaw dropped.

The intruder was opening the drawers in the refrigerator. The person was dressed from head to toe in black. A black beanie was pulled over the person's hair, but Raina could see the silver ends sticking out.

Raina's heart hammered in her chest. "What are you looking for, Bucky?"

While most senior citizens were no match for a healthy thirty-year-old woman, her height and desperation might give Bucky the strength of a cornered lioness. And Raina's natural inclination wasn't to knock over one of her grandma's peers. After all, what if Bucky broke a hip?

Bucky swung around. Her face was puffy and swollen like she might have just woken from a snooze. Her eyes shifted around the kitchen, probably checking for an escape route. "Where's the hammer?"

Raina blinked. She didn't tell anyone the murder weapon was a hammer. Only the murderer would know this. She had assumed Miles's murderer was the former mayor, but it had been Bucky all this time. "Why did you kill Miles Lutz?"

Under the dim light from the single bulb in the kitchen, the shadows made Bucky's face look like the old crone who handed Snow White the red apple. "Miles kept hounding us and hounding us. He had to go."

Instead of sounding afraid, Bucky's reedy voice

grew more guttural as she spoke. She drifted closer to the countertop, where all the power tools were charging.

Sweat popped up on the small of Raina's back. Heat engulfed her, along with fear. Her legs tensed, ready to dodge anything Bucky might hurl in her direction. "How did you get him to the house?"

Even though Bucky was taller than both Raina and her grandma, she would have to be a bodybuilder to lug Miles's dead body from another location to the house.

"It was easier than you think. I told Miles I had information to convict my husband. He was more than happy to meet me here. He thought I was finally the break he was looking for," Bucky said.

Raina grimaced. Oh, the poor man. If only he had kept the appointment with Chase McKenna instead. Not only would Miles be alive, but he would also have gotten the evidence he needed for his story. "How did you get his body inside the walls? Did someone help you?"

"Why because I'm a woman?" Bucky sounded offended.

"No. I wouldn't have known what to do," Raina said, trying to smooth things over.

"That's because you're a weak female. You just want to cook, clean, and mind babies," Bucky said, rolling her eyes. "My daddy owned a construction company, and I worked on a house every summer with him while I was in college."

Raina blinked. This was the first time a woman had called her a "weak female." Should she be offended? And why did she care what a killer thought of her? She resisted the urge to check her phone. Where was Joanne?

Bucky's hand snaked out toward the countertop. She grabbed a Dewalt battery and flung it in Raina's direction.

Raina ducked, but the battery caught her on the shoulder. Pain ran down her left arm like it was on fire. She blinked back the sudden tears. Why did she worry about hurting the little old lady?

Before Raina could straighten, Bucky grabbed the nail gun and swung around. Her finger squeezed the trigger.

Pop! Pop! Pop!

Raina dove to the floor, using the kitchen island as a shield. Her slick hands dropped the flashlight, and it clanged against the linoleum floor. As she lunged to grab her only weapon, her purse fell and spilled out. Her cell phone flew across the floor and disappeared from view.

Pop! Pop! Pop!

"Sorry about your phone. I can't have you calling for help," Bucky said.

Raina's hand tightened on the flashlight, and she grabbed the credit card tool the Science Ninjas had created for her. Help was already on the way. She only needed to stay alive long enough for Joanna to come with her blazing gun.

She hoped her grandma stayed asleep in the car. The last thing she needed was to worry about her grandma's safety when she was trying to survive.

Pop! Pop! Pop!

Nails dotted Raina's purse and the surrounding area, sticking up from the linoleum like the back of a porcupine. Her eyes widened at the sight, and her breath came out in jagged puffs. Heat rose and engulfed her face. She was a sitting duck.

If she ran, Bucky would spray nails across her back. But Raina couldn't stay huddled against the kitchen island because Bucky might just come around the corner. Why hadn't she prepared for this confrontation?

Raina had been too cocky—first, with Detective Sokol and now, with Bucky. She had probably secretly assumed she could handle the senior citizen.

Raina crawled to the opposite end of the island. Her left arm was numb. She held out the card tool like a mirror, hoping the reflection might show her Bucky's location on the other side of the kitchen. She tilted the card back and forth. No Bucky.

A scraping and rustling sound drifted over. What was Bucky doing? Was she still looking for the hammer now that she had Raina cowering behind the kitchen island?

Raina's hands shook, and she took a deep breath, hoping to calm herself. The air smelled of sawdust and stale air and a twinge of rose and musk perfume, which almost made Raina gag. The scent was too close for comfort. Where was the killer?

The fine hair on the back of Raina's neck stiffened. She glanced around either side of her again but didn't see anyone. Her blood roared in her ears. The sense of being watched was so strong that she glanced around again. With deep foreboding, she glanced up.

Bucky studied Raina from on top of the kitchen island. The nail gun was pointed right at Raina's face. Fear rose and clogged Raina's throat. She couldn't even scream.

The back door flung open. The war cry of a banshee filled the entire kitchen. Bucky swiveled to the door. A tablet flew like a Frisbee and whacked Bucky on the shoulder. She cried out in pain.

Raina rose from the floor. She swung the metal flashlight and knocked the nail gun away. Po Po rushed into the kitchen and blasted Bucky in the face with pepper spray.

Bucky jerked back. For a split second, she teetered on the edge of the countertop. Her eyes widened, and her arms swung out to grab hold of something. Her hands only grasped air. And she fell to the linoleum floor.

She lay on her side, huddled in the fetal position. From the strained look on her face, she must have broken something during her fall.

As Raina backed away from the countertop, she kept her eyes on the murderer. While Bucky might be down at the moment, there was no telling if she would get up again.

"Rainy, are you okay?" Po Po called out. Her voice was taut with tension.

"I think so," Raina said.

Po Po opened a cabinet door and grabbed the roll of paper towels. She pulled off several sheets and held it out. "Here, hon, press this on your shoulder until the paramedics come."

Raina glanced down. Her entire left side was covered with blood. The battery must have made a gash in her shoulder, but she had been too focused on surviving to notice. Her grandma's image blurred, and the room spun.

As if from the end of the tunnel, Raina could hear footsteps next to her ear. Someone spoke to her grandma. The woman's voice sounded familiar.

Raina opened her eyes to see her grandma pressing paper towels on her shoulder. Joanna was kneeling next to the killer.

"Help me! These two crazy women kidnapped me," Bucky pleaded, cradling her arm across her chest. "They dislocated my shoulder."

"The paramedics are on their way. Can you sit up?" Joanna asked.

"Yes, I can do it with your assistance," Bucky said. Her voice was honeyed, and it grated in Raina's ears.

"We didn't kidnap you, you deranged psycho," Po Po said. "She tried to kill my granddaughter."

Joanna still had her back turned to Raina, so she couldn't tell if the police officer believed Bucky.

"She came here looking for Miles's murder weapon." Raina cringed at how shaky her voice sounded.

"Please keep them away from me, Officer," Bucky said. "Bonnie Wong is upset that I will not support her bid for the social committee chair. That's why they kidnapped me. They were trying to convince me to change my mind." She scowled at Raina and her grandma. "They are the crazy ones."

Po Po tried to get up. "Why you—"

Raina jerked her grandma back down. "Wait for backup."

Po Po shook off Raina's hand. "You can lie all you want, but the cameras don't lie."

Bucky's face warped from innocent senior citizen to hateful villain. She launched for Joanna's service belt, grabbing at the gun holster.

Joanna's hands whirled.

Crack!

Bucky screamed, falling to the floor again, clutching her wrist. "My hand! My hand. You broke my hand."

The backyard lit up from multiple beams of flashlights. Footsteps approached the house.

"Police!" someone called out.

"Come on in," Joanna replied.

"Help! The officer broke my hand. This is police brutality," Bucky called out.

Several officers flooded the room with their guns drawn and flashlight blinding everyone. Once they assessed the situation, they put their weapons away. Joanna took charge of the situation.

By the time the emergency medical technicians came into the kitchen, everything had calmed down. One of them came over to help Raina, and the other checked on Bucky. Po Po tapped on the tablet—which only suffered a cracked screen—to pull up the video feed for an officer.

Joanna drifted over and watched Raina getting bandaged up. "You solved two cases in one night. I don't know if you're smart or stupidly lucky."

"Please don't tell Matthew," Raina whispered.

"No can do. You're a key witness."

Raina grimaced. "That's what I'm afraid of."

23

A HIDDEN ACE

A few days later, Raina was looking at tile samples with her grandma in the backyard of the house. True to his word, Chase had reimbursed them for the stolen items and approved their loan extension. Forrest had returned home later in the evening to find his father waiting for him in the bedroom. And like all good fathers, he had marched his son to the police station and then straight to rehab.

Blue and his crew were in the living room, adding a new beam before removing the wall studs. The driveway was taken over by a dumpster, and the front yard by several stacks of lumber and a table saw. Piles of sawdust covered the already patchy lawn. It was a disaster zone and perfectly orchestrated by her brother-in-law.

Raina's cell phone rang, and she pulled it out of her purse. She frowned at the number and let go to voicemail.

"Who is it?" Po Po asked.

"It's the Building Permit Counter," Raina said. "I guess my public records request is ready for pick up."

Po Po rolled her eyes. "Our tax dollars at work."

Raina laughed. She could afford to be in a good mood. Literally. Phil had given her a twenty-thousand dollar check for the capture of his brother's murderer this morning. She didn't need Red Bull to give her wings.

Footsteps crunched on the side yard. "Raina, are you here?" Joanna called out.

Raina gave the samples to her grandma. "Yes, I'm back here."

"I'll make tea," Po Po said. "We have about fifteen minutes, and then we need to leave for the senior center. I don't want to be late for the acceptance speech."

"They haven't even announced the final vote count yet. You don't want to put the horse before the cart," Raina said. She was afraid her grandma would be disappointed at the outcome for the social committee chair.

Po Po winked. "Even if I lose, I still have another ace up my sleeve."

As Raina watched her grandma stroll through the backdoor, a sense of foreboding filled her. Po Po sounded entirely too confident for Raina's comfort. Her grandma was up to no good.

Joanna came into view. "It looks like a disaster zone

out there. Are you sure you don't want to wait until Matthew comes back first?"

"What do I need him for? I have his brother," Raina said. While neither Matthew nor Blue spoke of the Las Vegas family reunion, she had found out their dad expected a full recovery.

Joanna grinned. "Too bad he's already married. Anyways, I want to let you know that I spoke to the deputy chief about Youri blackmailing Matthew. He's not happy about the whole thing. Matthew seems to be off the grid, so can you ask your husband to call his boss back ASAP?"

Raina's eyes widened. She didn't expect this. "Sure thing."

Matthew had already wrapped up the fieldwork portion of his side gig in Las Vegas. He would still have to spend the next few days briefing everyone and writing up his reports, but he should be home soon. However, her husband had wanted the time off to focus on the house construction. She wasn't sure he would be happy with the news.

"What will happen to Sokol?" Raina asked. No more detective for the traitor. He didn't deserve the respect.

Joanna's smile widened even more. "Last I heard, management is going through his application with a fine-tooth comb to verify his experience. They could take away his promotion if he lied. We'll have to wait and see."

Raina shook her head. "What about Bucky Brown? Did you find out why she killed Miles?"

"She did it to protect her husband's rising career. He had his eyes on the governor's office after all."

"I don't remember there being a governor candidate from our town."

"There wasn't one. Once Bucky told her husband what she did, he retired from politics. He couldn't run for any office after the murder without it being an albatross around his neck. It was bound to come out under media scrutiny."

Raina grimaced. Not only did Bucky murder an innocent man, but she killed her husband's career, too. "It backfired on her. I wonder what their marriage was like after something like this."

"By the way, congratulations on the new job," Joanna said.

Raina blinked. What new job? "Excuse me?"

"Didn't your grandma tell you? They just announced it at the Board meeting this morning."

Raina's heart stopped for a heartbeat and sped up. What did her grandma do now? "I don't know what you're talking about."

"You're the new director for the senior center."

"What happened to the old director?"

"She had to resign. The money is gone."

"Weren't there more candidates for the position?" Raina asked. While the director position was part-time, it held a lot of political power in their small community because of the influence over the senior citizen population.

"Yes, but a couple dozen senior citizens showed up at the meeting, vouching for you. I don't know how you did it, but you got them eating out of your hand."

Raina's face froze. For a second, she wondered if she had the deer in headlights look. She was her grandma's ace. No wonder Po Po wasn't worried about losing the vote for the social committee chair. "I get to play referee every day between my grandma and her arch-nemesis."

Joanna burst out laughing. "Good luck with that."

THE END

PLEASE REVIEW my books at your *book retailer*. As an indie author, reviews help other readers find my books. I appreciate all reviews, whether positive or negative.

Fair Cronies and Felonies
(Raina Sun Mystery #10)

ACKNOWLEDGMENTS

A story is a dream that a writer brings to life on paper. But a book needs a team to nurture it into the enjoyable tale you've just read.

I want to thank my editors, Alicia S. and Brandee, for wrangling my words so they are coherent.

And then, there are my wonderful beta-readers—Joyce S., Cindy I., Della D., Susan J., and Debi P.—thank you, ladies, for volunteering your time to catch these sneaky typos and grammatical errors.

And finally, thank you, Susan C. for the awesome cover.

I wouldn't have been able to bring this story to life without all of you, wonderful ladies. Thank you!

—Anne R. Tan

ALSO BY ANNE R. TAN

Thanks for reading *Chilly Comforts and Disasters.* I hope you enjoyed it!

Want to know about new releases, sale pricing, and exclusive content?

Sign up for Anne R. Tan's Readers Club newsletter at http:// annertan.com/newsletter

Your information would not be sold or transferred. Thank you for trusting me with your email.

Want More Raina Sun?

Raining Men and Corpses (Raina Sun #1)

Gusty Lovers and Cadavers (Raina Sun #2)

Breezy Friends and Bodies (Raina Sun #3)

Balmy Darlings and Death (Raina Sun #4)

Sunny Mates and Murders (Raina Sun #5)

Murky Passions and Scandals (Raina Sun #6)

Smoldering Flames and Secrets (Raina Sun #7)

Hazy Grooms and Homicides (Raina Sun #8)

Chilly Comforts and Disasters (Raina Sun #9)

Fair Cronies and Felonies (Raina Sun #10)

How about another series by Anne R. Tan?

JUST SHOOT ME DEAD

As the trill of the seldom-used ring tone filled the air, Lucy Fong jerked in her seat like someone had stabbed her rear with a needle, and the dumpling squirted out of her chopsticks, smacking into her date's glasses. It slid down his shirt before disappearing under the table, leaving a trail of grease and disappointment in its wake. She closed her eyes, wishing for a wormhole to open up beneath her feet.

In the last sixteen years, her estranged mother had only called her once, and that was when Lucy's stepfather had died. What bad news heralded the call this time? If it were good news, her half-sister would have posted it on social media by now. The conversation in the Chinese restaurant didn't miss a beat, and the clatter of eating utensils scraped against plates continued unabashed. Lucy's world had tilted on its axis, and no one had noticed.

Lucy opened her eyes, smiling like Miss America

on steroids. "Sorry. At least it wasn't red wine." She was supposed to have dinner with just her grandma this evening but had accepted the extra dinner companions —a nice Chinese doctor and his mama—with grace. This wasn't the first set-up, but it would be the last. Her cell phone vibrated to indicate Mom had left a voicemail.

"I've gotten a drink thrown in my face, but never a dumpling." The doctor wiped his glasses, smearing the grease across the lens. "I'm always up for new experiences."

Lucy's smile wobbled. Ah, a man with a sense of humor. A rare commodity these days. Too bad this was like everything else in her life—the timing was off. She was still working with her therapist to fix the clock. "It must be rewarding to save people every day."

"I don't help people because it's rewarding. I help people because it's the right thing to do," the doctor said, sounding like he believed every word.

Lucy groaned inwardly. A do-gooder. He was definitely too good for the likes of her. She wasn't a "bad girl" by any stretch, but she certainly wasn't an ideal wife for a Chinese doctor from a long line of Chinese doctors. She snorted. She pitied the poor woman who did meet those ideals.

The doctor's mama scowled at Lucy. She probably wanted a nice Chinese girl for her precious boy and got a half-Chinese girl instead. The woman had insisted on speaking in Cantonese during the entire meal and giving Po Po pointed looks whenever Lucy stumbled over the words with her thick American accent. "I guess you're not much use in the kitchen if you can't even handle chopsticks."

"Lucy is an internet whizbang. Maybe she could help advertise your son's business?" Po Po said.

The doctor's mama stiffened. "That wouldn't be necessary."

Lucy wanted to slap money on the table for the meal and walk out the door. She didn't need this after a full week of work. But her grandma was all the family she had left...or all the family she wanted in her life. She glanced at Po Po, and the hopeful look on her grandma's face fizzled out.

Po Po filled the awkward silence with chatter about a murder investigation. Her grandma had recently cut off her long silver braid to favor a short pixie cut with pink streaks much like Lucy's. When Po Po got to the car chase in her story, Lucy tuned her out. Her grandma read too many mystery books as far as Lucy was concerned. The matriarch of the Wong family should have been Irish for all the gab she spun.

Lucy snorted, earning another dark look from the doctor's mama. Speaking of mothers, she better see what Mom wanted.

"Sorry, I need to take this call. It's from my mother," Lucy said, pushing back her chair.

Po Po's eyes widened with concern, and she bit her lower lip as if to stop herself from saying something. She knew all about Lucy's tenuous relationship with her mother and half-sister.

"It's fine. We're done here," the doctor's mom said, dabbing at her lips with the cloth napkin.

Lucy thanked the doctor for a lovely dinner and shifted her gaze to Po Po. "I'll wait for you outside." She stumbled out of the restaurant, her heart pounding at the rejection from the doctor's family and the bruise to her ego.

The fog snaked around the red lanterns hung on the streets for the Chinatown tourists. Lucy shivered, but not from the chilly November night. Her hands shook when she pulled her cell phone from her purse. She tapped on the screen to listen to the voicemail, but instead of Mom's voice, the caller identified herself as Cousin Estelle.

YOUR MOTHER IS IN THE HOSPITAL. A NEIGHBOR FOUND HER SHOT IN THE STOMACH AT HER PRIVATE INVESTIGATION OFFICE. LUCY DEAR, YOU NEED TO COME HOME.

Her hands became numb, and the cell phone slipped onto the sidewalk. This couldn't be happening...

From behind her, she heard Po Po say goodnight to their dinner companions. Lucy swallowed the urge to throw up. Hurling the dumplings on the sidewalk would kill her reputation. The doctor's mama would make sure everyone knew Po Po's granddaughter was either a drunk or drug addict. San Francisco might be a big city, but Chinatown was a small community.

"Are you okay? What did your mother want?" Po Po said, rubbing Lucy's hunched back.

"It was her cousin. Mom is in the hospital," Lucy whispered, swallowing at the catch in her voice.

Po Po's lined face closed in like a flower petal. "Let's get you home, so you can pack to leave in the morning." She scooped up the cell phone and its battery off the sidewalk. "Broken. Why am I not surprised?" She tucked the phone into her purse. "Lucky you. I have a spare prepaid phone."

They strolled toward the brick three-story building two blocks away. The first floor housed the Fong Chinese Herbal Shop that once belonged to Lucy's deceased uncle. His apprentice ran the shop for her now. They got into the elevator, and Po Po hit the button for the third floor.

The keys rattled in Lucy's hand, and it took her three tries before she could open the door to her small apartment. She had lost a bedroom in the elevator renovation for the building, but it had been worth it. Her uncle had stayed in his home in the apartment across the hall until the end six months ago.

Once inside her small apartment, Po Po bustled around making tea in the plain terra cotta set her uncle had given her. The little ritual seemed out of place, given the gravity of the news, but comforting at the same time. Her uncle had done the same ritual when Lucy had shown up on his doorstep as a teenager in the middle of the night.

She glanced at the lucky cat clock on the wall with

its plastic swaying tail. Eight thirty. If she left now, she might make it to the hospital by one in the morning. She glanced out the window. The thick fog hid the building next door, except for one speck of glow that might have been a window. Maybe it would be closer to two in the morning by the time she rolled into Morro Cliff Village, a small coastal hamlet on the Central Coast.

It would make more sense to leave in the morning and be much safer for a woman traveling alone. But what if Mom didn't make it through the night? Though they no longer had a close mother-daughter relationship, they once did. She blinked at the tears burning in the back of her eyes. She was going to be too late...

Po Po wrapped Lucy's hands around a steaming cup of tea. "It's only too late when you give up. We can swing by my house on the way out of the City. I can pack a bag in less than ten minutes."

When Lucy's late uncle had taken her in, this generous woman had claimed Lucy as one of her own, welcoming the angry teen into the Wong family all those years ago. She would do anything for this woman, but this wasn't the kind of road trip for Po Po to tag along.

"I want to go alone. I need the time to think," Lucy said.

"You can't drive like this. You're still in shock," Po Po said.

Lucy shook her head. "I'm fine. It's just...I thought there would be more time."

The fluorescent lights flickered overhead, casting a sick gray pallor over the hospital room despite the cheerful yellow walls. The lights were dim, and the room was only big enough to hold the hospital bed and chair. On the wall opposite the entrance was a tall and narrow window like the kind found in a medieval castle and a door that led to the bathroom. The only sounds in the room were the beeping and whirring machines that kept Mom alive.

Lucy stood with her hands tucked under her armpits at the footboard of the hospital bed, mesmerized by her mother's still form. She didn't recognize the woman in front of her. The mother in Lucy's memory was a tall and willowy woman with thick blonde hair. Lucy had inherited her Chinese father's black hair and the Fong family's love for pastries. She considered it a small miracle she still had the metabolism of her youth.

Mom had teased Lucy for being such a serious and reserved child. Whereas, Mom had been a vibrant woman, expressive and passionate, using her entire body when she moved or spoke. Or at least she did years ago. The elderly woman in front of Lucy had a permanent frown in her rail yard of a face. Her body was more shrunken than lush, and the blonde had become a mane of white. The years since her stepfather's death had been hard on Mom, and it showed.

Lucy willed herself to feel something, but there was

nothing. The long drive in the dark had shuffled the fear into a corner. There was no sadness, no pain. Sure, Mom had chosen her husband and half-sister over Lucy, but that was a long time ago. Water under the bridge according to her therapist. And the anger had disappeared when her stepfather had died.

She just felt tired...and numb. Before the clumsy blind date, it had been a long day in the office, and her manager had screamed at Lucy for a data entry typo from a co-worker who was still on probation. Granted, as an internet marketing consultant, a single digit on a spreadsheet could kill an ad campaign, but it wasn't a gunshot wound.

Cousin Estelle slept awkwardly on the chair in the corner, her head leaning against the wall. She was actually her mom's younger cousin and in her mid-fifties. She had been a slender woman with too big front teeth and large ears when Lucy had left town. She had also been the unlucky recipient to inherit Great-grandma's first name. While she couldn't do anything with her teeth, her long dyed blonde hair hid the ears. Unfortunately, she had also grown in girth to match them.

Estelle jerked in her sleep and caught herself in time to keep from falling off the chair. She rubbed her sleepy hazel eyes and blinked at Lucy. She paused as if movement might make Lucy disappear.

"Thanks for calling me," Lucy whispered.

Estelle leapt off the chair and swept Lucy into a hug. Like the rest of the women in the Faye's side of the family, Estelle towered over Lucy at close to six feet tall. "It's so good to see you again." She pulled away, studying Lucy from head to toe. "Wow, you've grown into a little cutie pie."

Lucy raised an eyebrow. Little? In Chinatown, she had been as tall as most of the Chinese men at five foot six. She shook the random thoughts from her head. She wasn't here for a homecoming. "What happened?"

"I told you everything I know. You might want to talk to Max DeWitt later this morning. He's the town police chief now," Estelle said.

Lucy blinked. The last name DeWitt sounded familiar, and obviously, Estelle believed Lucy should remember him. "Did you talk to the doctor?"

Estelle shook her head. "Max tracked me down after your mom came out of surgery. The doctor makes his rounds in the morning around nine or ten. The nurse said your mother's condition is stable."

Lucy exhaled in relief. Stable sounded good. Maybe Mom would be back on her feet in a day or two, and Lucy could go home. "I can stay here if you want to go home."

Estelle held out a set of keys. "Why don't you go home and get some sleep? You have a long day ahead of you. I can't find your sister, and there wasn't anyone else..." She took a deep breath. "Do you want me to call a cleaning service for the office?" The words tumbled out in a nervous rush.

Lucy stiffened, trying to stop the shiver down her spine at the mention of the private investigation office.

How much blood... She slammed a lid on the thought. "I'll deal with it later. Let me give you the number to my prepaid phone. It's a temporary loaner." She dug in her purse and came up with a receipt. She wrote down the number for her grandma's spare cell phone.

Estelle tucked the slip of paper into her bag. "After you settle in, maybe we can have dinner or..."

Lucy grabbed the spare keys and stumbled toward the door. Settle in? She wasn't staying. "Thank you for everything," she said over her shoulder. She couldn't stand another minute of the whirling machines.

In her haste, Lucy didn't see the man on the other side of the threshold. She stepped on his toe, and her head rammed into his chest. She would have fallen if he hadn't grabbed onto her forearms.

When Lucy straightened, she suppressed a sigh. Could this day get any worse?

"Max," Estelle said. Her voice brightened at his appearance. "This is Lucy Fong, Dahlia Faye's...uh...daughter."

Lucy ground her teeth. Estelle was about to say bastard daughter. She couldn't believe people still remembered—or cared—that she was born out of wedlock. She shouldn't have come back. There wasn't anything she could do for her mother. She would only get insulted and shunned as she did in her childhood for being different. For having black hair among those with blonde or brown hair. For having slightly slanted eyes—

"Miss Fong, can I get you some coffee or tea?" Max

DeWitt asked, his face concerned. "You seem to be in shock."

Lucy shook off his hands. "I'm fine. I need to go." Edging around Estelle and Max, she backed out of the room. Neither of them moved to stop Lucy, but she ran like the past might catch up with her.

The drive to Mom's three-bedroom Cape Cod house was a blur. One moment, Lucy was backing out of the parking spot of the hospital, and the next she was on the gravel path in front of the house, breathing in the salt air. She couldn't remember if she blew through stop signs or sped through the small waterfront downtown area. It was a good thing the shops weren't open for business yet.

When Lucy opened the front door to let herself in, her hands shook and jiggled the keys. It had to be from hunger. She refused to believe a woman she hadn't seen for over a decade would have this kind of impact on her. After all, the phone call from Estelle had interrupted dinner. After she checked in the attic bedroom, she would fish out the granola bar in her purse.

As she made her way up the stairs, Lucy caught glimpses of the ocean through the windows. The pale moonlight sparkled over the dark water. Though the ocean was tranquil from this angle, she knew it crashed against the rocks below the cliff.

Her steps thudded loudly in the silent house. For a

moment, as the door to her old attic bedroom swung open, Lucy held her breath as if waiting for her half-sister to pop out from the closet. Of course, there was no chubby-cheeked preschooler. It had been sixteen years.

The room was just as she had left it—a twin bed against one wall, a desk next to a dormer window, and a small trunk against the far wall. The baseball bat was probably still underneath the bed. The posters of her teen idols curled on the edges, and the tape yellowed with age. Mom hadn't even cared enough to come up here to dust.

Continue Lucy's story.
Just Shoot Me Dead

ABOUT THE AUTHOR

Anne R. Tan is a *USA Today* bestselling author. She writes the Raina Sun Mystery series and the Lucy Fong Mystery series. Her humorous cozy mysteries feature Chinese-American amateur sleuths dealing with love, family, and life while solving murders.

Sign up for her newsletter for new release announcement, sales, and exclusive content at http://annertan.com/newsletter/